OF BIKES AND MEN

THE DEVIL'S OUTLAWS
BOOK 4

BETHANY DAWN

Editing by: Emi Janisch

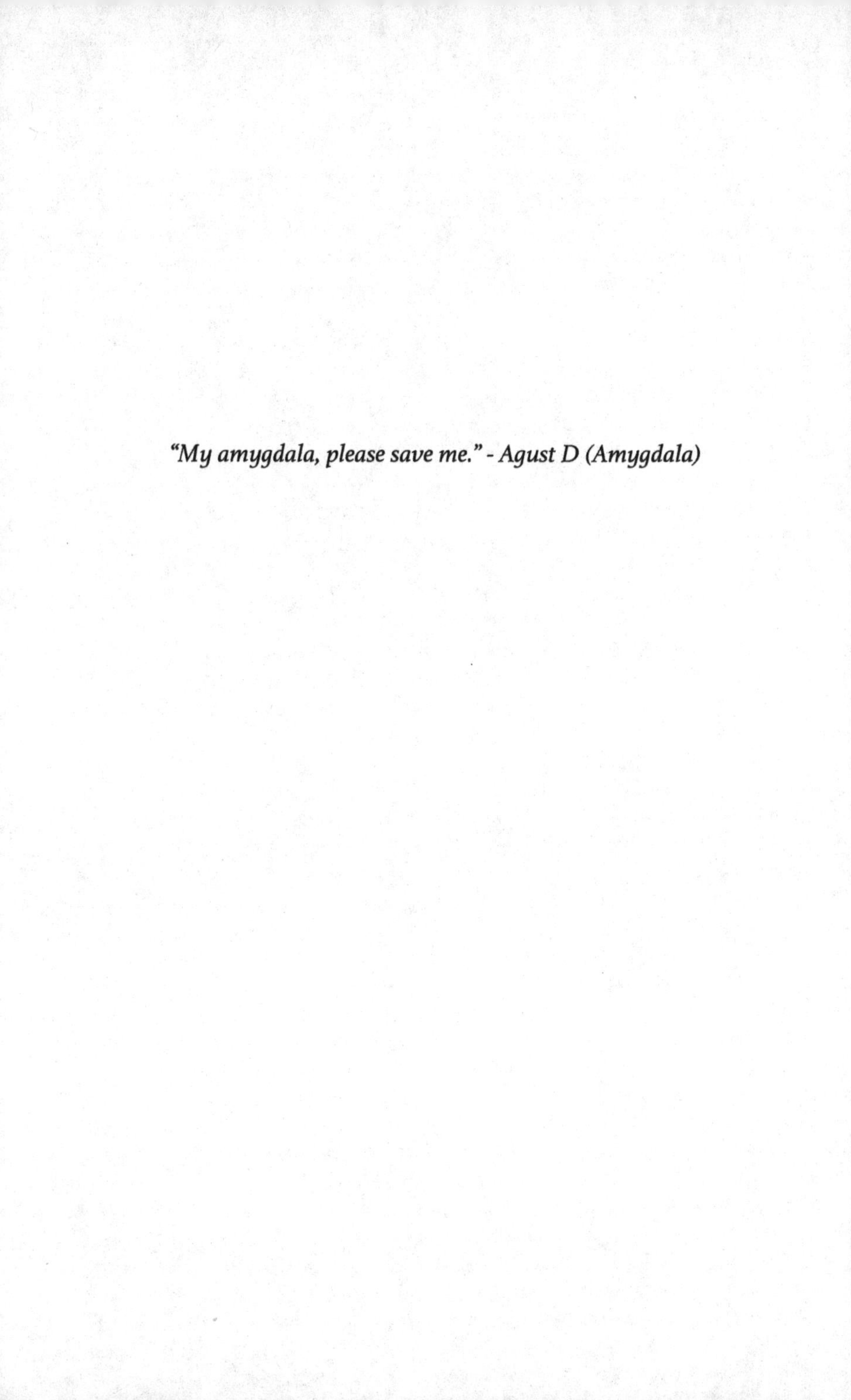

"My amygdala, please save me." - Agust D (Amygdala)

TRIGGER WARNINGS

This is a series about a 1%er motorcycle club, please expect them to act accordingly. Of Bikes and Men depicts grief, extreme acts of violence, murder, recreational drug use, torture, kidnapping, attempted sexual assault, and explicit group sex scenes. Please be conscious of your triggers, your mental health matters.

Bethany

PLAYLIST

AMYGDALA - Agust D
Time - NF
Double Take - dhruv
Haunted - Laura Les
this is how you fall in love - Jeremy Zucker, brent ii
Only - NF, Sasha Alex Sloan
I Think I'm In Love - Kat Dahlia
Paranoid - Chase Atlantic
moon and back - JVKE

MASON

Fuck. Fuck! My knuckles turn white on the handlebars as I open the throttle and speed down the road. My bike jerks unsteadily underneath me as I check behind me for the millionth time to make sure no one is following me.

Saint will probably already know where I ran to when he finds my room at the clubhouse empty, but I have nowhere else to go. At least, nowhere else where I could stay alive long enough to figure out who sent that video to Saint.

The heavy trees block out all sunlight and warmth and I slam on my brakes at the first gate, pressing the buzzer three times before I hear the audio click on.

"Miles, I need your help. It's life or death—mine, to be more specific. I'm not being dramatic, please let me in—" The gates rattle as they start to open, and I shut my mouth and hurry through the first gate, the second one already opening before I've even come to it.

My phone buzzes against my thigh and it takes me back to that night...

ONE MONTH AGO...

Leo and Jack are sparring in the ring, big smiles on their faces, even though Leo's is marred with the blood from his split lip. Crazy fucker. Nate and Tobi stand next to me, making jokes about the guys and shouting encouragement to them.

Another night, another club party, but this one is a little different—we're welcoming Finn and Huntley back from their honeymoon. It's so weird that he's married now. Reese and Cale are next... then who? It seems unlikely that Jack or Leo will hook up with someone. Maybe Wyatt. Definitely not Tobi or Nate. I don't know who the hell could put up with Saint's grumpy ass for longer than a few minutes, so that leaves Ronan—because my love life has been laughable, at best.

Joining the club has supplied me with no shortage of eager pussy, but none of them are... worth anything. All they care about is my patch and my bike. They don't care that I went to college; they don't care that I love having a big meal with my friends, or that I enjoy watching my brothers beat the shit out of each other for laughs. It's kind of lonely without an Old Lady.

Oh, speaking of the next one to get shacked up. My phone vibrates in my pocket and I pull it out to see Ronan's name on my screen.

"What's up, Prez?" I step away from the ring and move to an empty part of the lot so I can hear him over the music bumping through the compound.

"Something happened, kid, and I can't go into detail right now. Ugh, fuck!" he groans.

"Are you okay, Ronan?" I ask, my eyes darting to the table where Saint, Wyatt, Cale, Finn, and their girls are sitting.

Ronan inhales a shaky breath. "Shit, yeah. You're going to find out what happened soon, and I need you to do me a favor, Mason."

"Anything, Prez," I say, and I mean that with my entire being. I would do anything for this man and this club.

"You need to erase everything that happened tonight. Do not leave a single clue, and don't tell anyone."

I turn my back on the party and retreat into the trees at the back of the compound. "What's going on?" I ask, panicked.

"Do not tell anyone, Mason. Not even the club," his voice is so strained and weak.

"Prez..." I plead. I don't know what he's asking me to do, but it doesn't feel right.

"Promise me, Mason. Please."

"I promise, Prez." I lick my lips and look around at the dark trees, my mind racing. The line goes dead without a reply and I stay in the trees for a while, trying to figure out what Ronan meant. What is he asking me to erase? And where the hell is he? He's supposed to be here too.

Finally having enough, I head back to the party. I know I promised him, but maybe I can get some information from Cale about what the fuck is going on.

I clear the trees and walk back into the party. Saint is standing on the table he was sitting at before I walked back here. His head is jerking in every direction, like he's looking for someone, and Finn drags him off the table and holds his shoulders firmly, staring into his eyes. I don't know what they say, but I watch Finn's face fall. His brows pull together and his eyes glass over with tears as his arms drop to his side.

I know whatever Saint just told Finn is exactly what Ronan called me about. I know it's not good, and I'm fucked, because I just promised my President that I wouldn't tell any of my brothers what I'm about to mess with.

PRESENT...

I park my bike on the circle drive and take the wide steps up to the large, wooden door. Hitting the doorbell, I drag my hand down my face, sighing. I didn't even grab any clothes on my way out, just my hard drive—which, now that I think about it, probably looks suspicious, but I wanted to make sure Saint didn't destroy it in a fit of rage and lose any evidence I might have to clear my name. I left my phone at the clubhouse too, but not before texting Allie on a burner I had hidden in my bathroom. She said she would send me the video, but I know she's distancing herself right now. She doesn't know what to believe.

She didn't offer to come with me, just agreed to when I asked for the video. I don't blame her. If this were happening to someone else, I'm not sure I'd believe them, but I didn't kill Ronan.

The door finally opens to a short, brunette girl, and if it weren't for the distinctive house and the gates, I would think I was at the wrong place.

"Uhhhh..." I look beyond her, into the house, and then behind me. Who the hell is she? I've never seen anyone at this house but Miles and me. I've never even seen Cale here.

"Hi, I'm Briar," she says, offering me her hand.

I look down at it and then back to her soft face. "Is Miles here?"

"Miles?" Her arched brows knit together and she takes a step back. "Dox!" she yells behind her, and I see Miles rushing down the stairs.

Miles takes the door from the girl and opens it further. "Briar," he says, gesturing to her with his words to step aside.

"Who's Miles?" she asks, stepping aside and crossing her arms.

"That's my name." He grits his teeth, and I awkwardly walk between them, clutching the strap of my backpack.

"What else are you keeping from me?" she snaps, and my eyes bounce from one to the other.

"A lot." He looks down at her from the bottom of his eyes. Briar glares and runs her tongue over her lip. "What was life and death, Mason?" He turns his green gaze to me.

Uhhh…" My eyes flick between them once more, not sure what I should be sharing with Briar if Miles wasn't even sharing his real name.

"My office, I'll meet you there." I abruptly turn around and hurry for the hall, and when I look back, Briar and Miles are hissing whispers at each other.

I'm starting to think I should have taken my chances with Saint, because I have no clue what the fuck I walked in on here.

SAINT

"Saint, wait!" Allie yells, chasing after me as I leap from her front porch and stalk to my bike—Ronan's bike. Fuck!

I turn around and she stops abruptly, her chest brushing against mine. "For what, Allie?" I shout.

I watch her spine steel, l and if the circumstances were any different, I would feel bad for yelling at her, but the only thing I can think about right now is how many nights a murderer slept next to her. How close they became while I was too busy being a dick. If Mason could do this to his own club, there isn't any line he wouldn't cross. Allie looks around at the neighborhood, at the houses, and the people leaving their homes to start their workday. "You can't kill him." She keeps her voice even and reaches for my arm.

I jerk away from her as her words slice through me. "I am." I keep my glare on her as I straddle the bike Ronan and I spent months rebuilding and start it up, backing out of her driveway and tearing down the block.

I'm going to kill Mason—and Allie won't stop me—even if I lose her for it. I would rather her be safe than be with him, and I can't forgive what he did—none of the guys will be able to. We're going to hunt him down like an animal, and I won't stop until I'm dragging his lifeless body to Ronan's grave.

FOUR MONTHS AGO...

"Can you fucking believe that?" Ronan asks, leaning against the leg of the wooden table, his long legs extended in front of him as he sits on the rolling stool in his garage.

"Yes." I laugh and take a drink from the beer bottle in my hand. "We keep getting older and the club whores just keep staying the same age."

Ronan scoffs, shaking his head. "Shut the fuck up, you're only twenty-five!"

"And you're only thirty-five, but when you're fucking around with girls five years younger—well, fifteen in your case—you feel a little old," I counter.

He sighs and stands, grabbing a tool from the table he was sitting against. "I don't know what you're talking about, I haven't seen you mess with a club girl in months."

Leaning against the plush recliner, I watch Ronan return to the bike sitting in the middle of his garage—if you could even call it that right now. It's so disassembled, it could be a damn microwave for all I know right now. "Yeah, well, other things have been keeping my attention." Blonde hair fills my head. A black dress and pizza grease. Allie.

"You need to quit them girls anyways, Saint. Find someone and settle down, like Cale and Finn." Metal tinks as he messes with some part of the bike, his hands drenched in black grease.

"Kind of hypocritical, don't you think, Ro? I haven't seen you with anyone serious in years." I lean against the chair and watch Ronan work. We do this every weekend; sit in his garage and drink and talk shit. Other than texting or seeing Allie, it's the only thing I look forward to.

He shakes his head, smiling softly as he focuses on what he's working on. "The club is my Old Lady. I got enough on my plate with all of you shitheads and our four new kids."

"Wyatt's not a kid," I muse.

"No," Ronan laughs. "He's not."

Standing up, I toss my bottle in the recycling bin and grab another for the both of us. "How'd you guys meet, anyways?"

Ronan takes the bottle from me, brushing my fingers when we trade the beer. "We went to high school together—"

"During the stone ages?" I joke.

"Fuck you." Ro chuckles. "When he got out of the military and was lost on what to do with his life, I took him in."

Landing in the chair deftly, I notice the black stains on the tips of my fingers. "Typical Ronan, always bringing in strays." I wipe the grease off of my fingers and onto my jeans. Asshole.

"It's how I met you." He reminisces, his voice drifting like he's remembering our meeting. His eyes snap up to mine and the sincerity in them holds me hostage. Ronan is like my father, brother, and best friend, all rolled into one. Which means he's really fucking important to me. In fact, he's been the most important person in my life for almost all of my adulthood. He's been my rock, always there for me through whatever I needed. "Don't run the club like I have."

"What do you mean?" I lean forward, dropping my legs on either side of the raised recliner and resting my elbows on my thighs.

"Alone." The word hangs in the air like lead, and I brush it off because of how many beers we've had.

"You don't have to worry, brother. I'm not letting you leave this club without me." I push off of my thighs and lounge back on the chair.

PRESENT...

Punching in the code for the compound gate, my heart beats

wildly in my chest—tapping out such a rough rhythm that my chest hurts. As soon as the gate is open wide enough for my bike to fit through, I gun the throttle and rush into the lot, driving right up to the door and leaving the baby blue bike.

The warm, summer air has nothing on the heat of the hatred that is running through my veins as I yank the door to the clubhouse open and storm in.

"Where the fuck is Mason?" I shout at the top of my lungs, my yell echoing through the empty clubhouse.

A cut slut flinches behind the bar at the boom of my voice, and two others huddle together on the couch against the wall, their silent tears streaming down their faces as they stare at me with wide eyes. What the fuck happened here?

Jack strides out of the kitchen with a pink-tinged paper towel, drying off his hands, and I look between everyone. "What happened and where is Mason?"

"Someone dropped Peyton off at the gate, beaten. Nox took her to the hospital, and Mason left pretty quickly afterward," Jack says, tossing the paper towel into the trash and grabbing a bottle of water from one of the fridges.

For one fucking day could things just not implode? "Fuck!" I shout, banging my fist on the nearest table and making the girls flinch again. "Where did Mason go?"

Jack shakes his head while he swallows his drink, completely unfazed by any of this. He's a lot like me—always composed—at least the me that I was before I met Allie and actually started feeling shit. "I don't know, Prez. He took off in a hurry and didn't say anything. I figured he was going back to Allie."

I scrub my hand over my eyes. Too much is going on right now. Peyton and Mason. "I'll call Finn and he can handle Peyton, I've got to find Mason," I growl, turning around to leave.

"What's going on, Prez?" Jack asks, his voice ringing clearly, and the word "Prez" ricocheting in my head, setting my anger off again.

Stopping, I take a deep breath and say it. "Mason killed Ronan." I look over my shoulder and see the first time that Jack's composure breaks. Confusion, anger, and sadness flash across his face quickly before he pulls himself back together and his spine straightens as he waits for me to do something, or say something, but there isn't anything else to say.

I leave the clubhouse, the door banging off the wall with the force, and I straddle my bike, dialing Finn.

"What's up, Prez?" Finn answers immediately.

"I need you at the clubhouse, now," I grit through my teeth. Every second that the piece of shit is still breathing is grating on my nerves. Rage courses through me, making my hands shake with the need to drain the life out of Mason.

"On my way," he says, always my loyal VP.

"Wait." I stop him. "I won't be here when you get here, so I need to fill you in now."

Finn pauses slightly before answering. "What's going on, Saint?"

"Peyton was found beaten at the gate. Nox took her to the hospital, and I don't know anything else. I need you to figure out how she is and what happened."

"Got it," Finn cuts me off.

I blow out an angry breath. "There's more."

"Shit." Finn sighs.

I take a deep breath and steel myself for having to replay this morning. "I got a video this morning of Mason killing Ronan."

My confession hangs in the air, and Finn takes a long time to answer. "What do you mean?"

"I mean someone sent me a surveillance video from the alley where Ronan died, and it showed Mason shooting him," I snap, shouting at Finn.

"Wait for me at the clubhouse." I hear the loud rumble of Finn's bike echo through the phone.

"No. I'm going to find him," I say, ready to pull the phone away from my ear and hang up on Finn.

"Saint!" Finn's voice booms down the line and I put the phone back to my ear. "This is a club issue and we need to figure it out as a club. Don't you think we would all want to be a part of avenging Ronan? He was our President too."

I snarl at him, but he's right. Ronan wasn't just my brother; he was brothers with everyone in this club. Everyone has the same types of stories about him that I do. Him saving them, taking them in, teaching them, loving them. As much as I want this for myself—need it—they do too.

"Fine, call everyone. This ends today," I growl, watching the gate open as Allie's Audi rolls through.

ALLIE

I know he didn't do it—he couldn't have—but the video… That was definitely him. Saint opened the video while I was laying on his chest, and we watched the entire thing together. Ronan walked into the alley, his head looking around swiftly, and then Mason followed shortly after him. Mason said something, Ronan turned around, and Mason shot him. Then once more, after he fell. And then he ran—leaving Ronan lying in the alley—before the video cuts off.

I chased Saint out of my house in my pajamas before he sped off. I knew I had to follow him, so I ran back inside for my car keys and some sandals I left by the front door the other day.

The gates slowly roll open and I drum my nails against the steering wheel impatiently. Saint is at the other end of the lot, sitting on his bike, and talking into his phone. No dead Mason in sight, so I guess he got out in time. I called him as I was running out of my house.

I park my car in front of Saint's bike and get out.

"Move the car, Allie!" Saint shouts.

"No!" I yell back, walking toward him.

He jumps off of his bike and pulls his cut off of his shoulders.

"Jesus Christ, Allie. Everyone here can see your fucking tits!" He drops his cut over my shoulders and the weight of it settles a small part of me. It feels like I'm wearing a bulletproof vest made completely out of Saint; his strength and power.

I look around at the empty lot but decide to let that go. "Well, I couldn't just go inside to take a shower and do my makeup while you ran off to kill Mason," I sass.

"This is a club issue, Allie." Saint narrows his eyes, his light hair falling forward as he looks down at me.

"Bullshit, Saint!" I step into his chest, setting my jaw in place. "You are not going to just run after him and kill him! Hear him out. You know him, you know this doesn't make any sense!"

Saint licks his lip and shakes his head, his eyes floating above me. "The only thing that's made sense since Ro died has been you, Allie." He looks at me again and the look in his eyes breaks my heart. He's been struggling for so long.

My hands fall on his waist and I grip his tee shirt in my fists, stepping into him. "Then listen to me. There's something else going on. Talk to him."

The loud rumble of a bike pulls up to the gate, and I look over my shoulder as Saint and I watch the gate slide open. Finn sits on the other side. "We have Church, Al. Go home, I'll call you after."

I turn back to him, my eyes narrowing. "You really think I'm going to do that?"

He sighs and drapes his arm over my shoulder, pulling me into his side. "No," he says as he walks us toward the clubhouse.

MASON

"WHAT'S SO DAMN IMPORTANT?" MILES SNAPS, THE DOOR slamming into the wall as he barges into his office.

"Who's the girl?" I ask, leaning forward to rest my elbow on the desk and prop my chin on my hand.

Miles narrows his eyes at me as I stand from his chair and pull up one beside it to sit in. He's always so territorial and snappy. "She's no one." He rolls his eyes and walks to his chair.

"I've never seen you with a girlfriend," I press, trying to get some idea of who she is. I really have never seen him with anyone. He doesn't talk about his personal life much. He doesn't even leave his house often. He's a loner.

Miles growls, the sound vibrating out of his throat and honestly, kind of scaring me. "She's not my..." he pauses. "Why the fuck are you here?" He turns to glare at me and I know that I should drop it. He's testy with Briar here.

I sigh and open the top drawer of the desk, hearing Miles's frustrated breath at my intrusion into his space. Taking out a cord, I plug it into my phone and then offer him the other end to plug into his computer. "I have to show you something."

Miles holds up one finger and stands from his chair, stomping to the door. He yanks it open and Briar almost falls into the room. Obviously, she was listening against the door, trying to eavesdrop. She stands and squares her shoulders, glaring up at Miles. "My office is soundproof, but nice try. Go away." He slams the door in her angry face and comes back to the desk.

He looks between me and the cord before taking it and plugging it in. A loading screen pops up before the video. Miles and I watch the security footage of me killing Ronan, and he turns to me when it's over. "What the fuck was that?" he asks calmly, his green eyes narrowed on me.

"Someone is framing me. I didn't do that." I point to the screen. "I was at the party at the clubhouse when that happened." I pause, looking to the floor so I don't have to see any judgment in Miles's eyes. I feel like shit for covering for Ronan, but he asked me to. Now it's biting me in the ass. "Ronan called me that night. He sounded like he was hurt and he told me to wipe everything and not tell anyone about it. I wiped the original security footage and wiped his phone." I look back up at the screen. The video stopped on me looking down at Ronan. Lying on the ground. A gunshot wound in his back. "This has to be a deepfake."

"Let's see." Miles turns away from me and downloads the video. He presses the play button again and makes the video full screen. Leaning in, he watches the video closely. "They did a really good job," he says after watching it a third time.

"Can you prove it's fake?" I ask, leaning back in my chair. I didn't watch the video again with Miles. It makes me sick to my stomach to see a fake version of myself killing my President. I would never. I only tried to help; to do what he asked.

"Maybe. I coded a program a few years ago that can detect if a video or photo file has been corrupted. I'll run it through that."

Miles leaves the video and pulls up a program, uploading the video to it.

This does, however, interest me, so I lean forward and watch as the video plays through on fast forward and code runs down a box on the screen. "How do you have all of these programs?"

"Clients." Miles leans back and watches the screen work. "I had a political candidate whose wife's face was put over a porno and released. The husband wanted to prove that it was fake."

I cock my head and turn to him. "Who do you work for?" He always has the weirdest stories about his work.

"Anyone who can afford me." Miles smirks as the video stops and another video pops up.

"What now?" I ask, looking at the screen, a little scared to watch the next video.

Miles turns in his chair and faces me. "If there were any alterations to the video, then the program can strip it and get the original. Are you sure you were at the party that night?"

"It wasn't me, Miles." I hold his eyes so he knows I'm genuine.

He nods once and turns back to his computer. "Then let's see who the bastard is."

Miles clicks play on the black screen of the video, and we lean forward to watch it together.

A man walks into the alley. Both of our eyes widen at the same time. "Oh, shit," Miles whispers.

MASON

WITH EACH TURN OF THE LOADING WHEEL, I CAN FEEL MY HEART beating faster and louder in my ears. My only chance at staying alive is to figure out who this guy is. I flick my eyes between my screen and Miles's. He's running the *real* guy from the video through facial recognition, and I'm trying to recover the original file from when I wiped it.

My phone vibrates on the desk next to my keyboard and I glance down at it. The only person who should have this number is Allie, and that's not her number on the screen. Fuck...

I reluctantly answer the call, but I don't say anything, waiting for him to be the first one to speak. "If you wanted to disappear, you probably shouldn't have given your new number to the girl-friend that we both share," Saint says down the line, and the lack of emotion in his voice sets a chill in my bones. He might be cold most of the time, but at least that's a normal emotion for him. This isn't.

"I'm not running, Saint. I didn't do it." I glance at Miles's screen again, begging for it to hurry the fuck up.

"You have one hour to get to the clubhouse. I'm letting you

plead your case, and we'll decide if you're guilty or not as a club."

Miles's eyes snap to mine and I know he heard that. I don't think he realized how serious I was when I said this was life or death. "How do I know you're not just trying to bait me?"

"I don't care about baiting you. I know where you are, and if you're not here in an hour, then we're going to hunt you down, and I'll tie you to the back of my bike, drag you to Ronan's grave, and slit your throat to water the grass. It's your choice. If you didn't do it, then I'll see you in an hour. If not, then I'll see you when you're tied to the back of my bike." He hangs up and a shudder runs up my spine.

"He's a creepy motherfucker," Miles drawls.

"He's serious." I point my finger at his screen. "So hurry up."

Finally, the files I had wiped come back, and I click into the surveillance footage to compare the video they sent and the one I have here. In hindsight, I shouldn't have completely wiped it— I should have kept a copy for myself—but I never thought someone would try to frame me!

Clicking on the video, I fast forward until I see Ronan walk into the alley. I click play, and then the screen goes black. What? I scroll through the feed—thinking it's an error on my part— and the video picks back up the next day. They deleted the entire night, and because I just deleted the entire thing, I never even looked. I didn't want to watch Ronan die, so I never watched it. Fuck.

"They erased it before I ever got to it," I say quietly, staring at the screen. That was my proof.

"They're covering their tracks, but that's fine, because we have the guy's name. Joseph Vasquez, a new member of Los Lobos, in and out of jail a few times for assault and theft." Miles leans back in his chair, linking his fingers behind his head. "I'd bet taking out Ronan was his initiation."

"What the fuck?" I sigh. "I know we just got an answer, finally, but I feel like all it did was open up more questions."

"Yeah." Miles licks his lips and stares at the screen, Joseph's most recent mugshot staring back at us.

I shut my laptop and slide it into my bag. "You know you have to come with me, right?"

Miles straightens up and turns to me. "What?"

"You're my witness that I didn't fake this video." Miles glances at the door with a look of pain, or maybe annoyance, crossing his face. "You can bring Briar," I offer, knowing where his mind has gone.

"This should be fun." Miles sighs heavily and pushes his chair back from the desk.

6

MASON

My hands slip on my handlebars as I pull into the compound. Nox watches me with his mouth in a flat line as I slowly drive through the gate. Allie's car is parked by the door to the clubhouse, and the sight both soothes the churning nervousness in my stomach and feels like a fist is squeezing my heart, all at the same time.

Seeing her makes me feel more at peace, but I don't want her to be here if things are going to go south. If my club doesn't believe that I didn't betray them.

I would die for my club, and today, I might.

Parking my bike, I step off and watch Miles park his Porsche. He gets out and closes the door, walking over to me. He clicks a button on his key fob before slipping it into the pocket of his black pants. Briar doesn't follow him, and I look between him and the car. She definitely came with us, and he followed me the whole way here.

"What?" he asks. "I left it running."

Oh my God… He locked her in the car. "She's going to kill you in your sleep." I chuckle, turning to walk to the clubhouse.

Miles's eyes turn to slits as he glares ahead. "She's already tried." He picks up his pace and walks ahead of me, leaving me staring at his back.

I bark out a laugh. I think he finally met his match.

Miles opens the door to the clubhouse and we walk in. My brothers are spread through the area—sitting and drinking—and all eyes fall on us as we step in. Everyone stops talking, and I lick my lips nervously as I look around at them. I can tell they don't know what to believe by the looks on their faces, except for Saint. Finn holds him still with a big hand wrapped around his bicep as he all but hisses at me. A furious rage dances in his ice-blue eyes, and I want to turn around and run as far as I can just from his look alone. But I didn't do this, and I need them to believe me.

My gaze falls on Allie last, and my heart breaks at the doubt in her eyes. I understand why she would be wary, but it still hurts that she would doubt me at all. She looks cautious as she sits on the barstool beside Saint, wearing his cut.

"In the Chapel. Now!" Saint booms, yanking his arm away from Finn and stomping toward the Chapel.

Everyone follows, with Allie, Miles, and myself making up the back of the trail of guys.

"I didn't do it, Solnyshko," I whisper behind her.

"Then prove it," she pleads over her shoulder, keeping her eyes forward.

My brothers file into the room and take their seats, and I shut the door and stop at the end of the table, looking over at my empty spot.

"Only brothers sit at this table, and right now, you're a dead man, so stay standing," Saint snarls. I look away from my chair to see Allie lingering behind Callum, looking around at the chairs. "Come here, my Queen, your throne is right here." Saint disregards me and pushes away from the table, offering her his hand.

I watch her take his hand and sit on his lap with absolutely no jealousy. I feel relief that he's finally let her in, and in front of the club. I just hope she'll give him a lot of grief if he kills me today.

"What the fuck is he doing here?" Nate snaps, pointing to Miles.

Miles glares back at Nate with one eyebrow raised, and I place an arm on his shoulder, hopefully letting him know to let it go. The last thing this situation needs is these two snapping at each other. "He's my witness."

Saint leans back in his seat, one hand fisted tightly on the arm of his chair, but the one wrapped around Allie rests lightly on her thigh, rubbing gently back and forth. "How do we know he isn't lying to us on your behalf?"

Miles sighs and drags his hand down his face. "Because I was working for Ronan, and I think what he was asking me to look into got him killed."

Everyone's heads snap to Miles, mine included. "You never told me," I say under my breath, but the room is so silent that I know everyone heard me.

Miles looks at me, a little softer than he looks at everyone else. "He told me not to tell the club."

"Let's get on with this, guys," Finn interrupts, and I startle out of my staring at Miles, turning back to the table.

"Where's Leo?" I ask, looking at his empty chair.

"He switched places with Nox and is with Peyton at the hospital. Jack has him on the phone," Cale offers, while Saint just continues to glare at me.

"Right," I murmur, remembering Peyton, beaten and lying at our front gate. Taking my laptop out of my bag, I place it on the table and turn it to face everyone. "Saint." I look up at him out of the top of my vision. "The video you got was real security footage from the alley, but it was altered to have my face over the guy. It's called a deepfake, and it's like Photoshop on fucking steroids." I pull up the original video, the one without my damn face in it. "This is the real footage. Miles has a program that can detect altered material and uncover the originals."

"Of course, he does," Cale sighs.

I look at Cale, but he doesn't look as pissed as the others, and he knows Miles, so he knows what he's capable of. "The man in the video is Joseph Vasquez. He's a new member of Los Lobos. I think——-"

"Ronan had me looking into Los Lobos and a club that they ran before he died. I think Joseph's initiation task was to take out Ronan, because they found out that he was looking into them," Miles interrupts.

"Why did Ronan ask you to look into Los Lobos and their club, and why did he want you to keep it from us?" Saint snaps.

Miles shrugs, not at all disturbed by Saint's anger. "I don't ask questions, I just get paid."

"Real stand-up fucking guy, aren't you?" Saint seethes. "Taking money and never knowing what your shit will mean for others."

Miles's brow raises again, and I know shit is close to hitting the fan. "Did you want me to ask questions every time your club came to me for help? Like what happened to Elijah Murphy?"

"Saint," Finn warns. "He did what our President asked, which is exactly what we all do."

"This is it?" Saint asks, still glaring at me.

"No." I click out of the video and pull up the satellite map. "This map shows that my phone was pinging here at the club before, during, and after Ronan's murder."

"You could have left your phone here," Tobi challenges.

"So I also pulled stoplight cameras to show that I never left the compound. Not until we all left together, after Saint got the call. Miles brought his laptop to run the footage through if you don't believe me." I play through the various routes one could take to get from the compound to where Ronan was found, watching Allie the entire time. If no one else believes me, I need her to know I'm telling the truth. I pull up Ronan's and my phone records next. "I got a call from Ronan right before Saint got the call. He asked me to wipe everything clean, but he wouldn't tell me what was going on and he asked me not to tell any of you."

"What the fuck is with all of these secrets!?" Saint booms and Allie flinches slightly on his lap. "I'm sorry," he says under his breath to her and she nods down at him. My fingers itch to reach out to her, to hold her against me and never let her go again. I can see she believes me, but I hope this is enough for Saint.

"I scrubbed the security footage without ever watching it, and I deleted his call to me from his phone. Miles and I went back to watch the security footage and someone else deleted the portion of the murder. That wasn't me."

"What do you think, Prez?" Finn asks.

I hold my breath as Saint looks up at Allie. She turns to look down at him and I watch so much pass between them. It's different seeing them interact in any other way than yelling and insulting each other. Last night was a huge step in the right direction, and then Los Lobos threw a bomb in it. "I don't think he killed Ronan." I release my breath and close my eyes. "But I'm still fucking watching you," he snaps. Thank fucking God! "What the fuck was Ronan looking into Los Lobos behind our back for?"

"Did you guys ever check his burner?" Miles asks casually.

"What fucking burner?" Finn asks.

"I have his burner, call it," Saint commands.

Miles shrugs and pulls his phone out of his pocket, and I

watch him pull up a contact named "R burn" and hit call. The room is quiet as we all look around at each other.

"What the fuck is going on?" Leo asks.

"Ronan had a second burner. I have his burner and it didn't ring," Saint says, with his usual annoyed look.

Cale looks Saint up and down. "Where's his burner?"

"Hidden," Saint says curtly, tapping Allie on her thigh.

"Where are you going?" Allie asks, standing.

Saint looks between her and me before answering. "To the alley to look for his burner." He walks past the table and me and out of the door.

Allie rushes behind him but stops at me instead of following him out of the door. She crashes into my chest and I hold onto her with all of my strength. "I knew you didn't do it," she says into my chest.

"Thank you." I kiss the top of her head, squeezing her tighter to me.

"For what?" I feel her kiss my chest.

I stroke her soft hair. I was so scared that I'd never get to do this again—hold her. "For believing in me. I love you."

"I love you too." She pulls away and leans up, pressing her lips to mine. I savor the feel of her. I'll never take it for granted again. She pulls away way too soon and I slowly open my eyes. "We should go with him."

I nod, reluctantly letting her go. "You're right."

A car alarm blares from outside and Miles sighs as the remaining brothers jump to their feet. "I have to go." Miles rolls his eyes and leaves the Chapel.

All of us are on high alert as we chase after Miles. With a hand on Allie's hip, I direct her behind me as we follow my brothers through the clubhouse. I know she's not going to stay put—not when Saint is outside with the alarm—so there's no point in trying to ask her to stay in here.

Allie rushes around me, and I pick up my speed to hurry after her. She pushes aside my brothers, forcing her way through the crowd and out the door.

"Dammit, Allie, at least let me go first!" I shout after her, but she ignores me and brushes past Finn and Jack.

Allie hurries toward Saint, and I slow and look around the compound. Everything is normal. The gates are closed, and Nox is standing guard by them. I continue to scan the parking lot and realize that the alarm is coming from Miles's car, which he is walking toward with a small brunette slung over his shoulder, his long legs eating up the parking lot quickly.

Chuckling to myself, I look over at Allie and Saint. He has his arm slung over her shoulders, holding her close as they watch the show that everyone else is watching. Miles wrangles Briar over his shoulder and then scolds her as he holds the passenger side door open for her and she climbs in.

Miles glares murderously as he walks around his car to get in on the driver's side. I am so confused about who Briar is and why they're together if they so clearly hate each other.

"We're going with you, Saint," Allie says as I make my way over to them. He opens his mouth, but Allie cuts him off. "I don't care what you say, we're going."

Saint sighs, adding a groan at the end. "Fine."

Rubbing my jaw, I hide my smile behind my hand. I'm enjoying bossy Allie way more than I should, especially when it comes at Saint's expense. But more so, I love that Saint is letting her in now. That he's allowing her to call the shots and be a part of this.

He straddles his bike and pulls it upright. "Get on, then."

Allie shakes her head and steps backward. "I'm riding with Mason."

Saint's eyes narrow to slits. "Get. On. My. Bike, Allie," he says through clenched teeth.

I lean over Allie's shoulder and speak into her ear. "It's okay, Solnyshko. Go ride with Saint."

She turns around, her head dropping back to look at me. "No. Saint is just throwing his big President dick energy around." Her pink lips form a slight pout and I hold myself back from nipping at her lips. Actually, fuck that. I'm not hiding how much I want my girl. I lean down and bite her bottom lip, sucking it into my mouth and enjoying the small squeal she lets out.

"I know." I pull away from her and wrap my arms around her waist. "But I don't care. You can ride on his bike now, as long as you ride my dick later." My breath ghosts over Allie's lips, and I watch as her pink tongue darts out to wet her lips before they slide into the sexiest smirk. God, this woman is everything that I've ever dreamed of. She's absolutely perfect, even on her worst day.

"Deal," she whispers.

I spin her around and pull her hair over her shoulders, dividing it in three sections and messily braiding it. "And to make things fair, Sainty can watch," I say loudly, nudging her forward and smacking her on the ass as she steps away from me.

Saint and Allie, Finn, Cale, and I leave the compound. The four of us make a diamond shape as we ride, with Saint at the head.

Ronan could not have picked a worse part of town to be doing shady shit in—to die in. He chose the only bad part of town, in an alley behind a liquor store that sells weed in the back. That's how we got lucky with the security footage. The shop keeps a camera above their back door for theft purposes.

We park at the mouth of the alley and slowly get off our bikes. "AMYGDALA" by Agust D echoes from the store and bleeds into the alleyway.

"Why do you think the burner is here?" Cale asks.

Saint stops at the exact spot where Ronan laid—where he... I'll never be able to get the visual of him bleeding out on the ground out of my head. I don't think Saint will be able to either. He stares down at the pavement, silent. Allie notices and walks to him, wrapping her arms around his stomach and resting her head on his back.

Saint clears his throat and looks up. "Because there wasn't another phone with his belongings from that night, or at his house. It has to be here." He pulls Allie's hands off of him but doesn't let go of her as he looks around. "It has to be near here. He only came this far in the video." His ice-blue eyes scan the ground and the wooden pallets stacked against the dingy, white, brick building, before stopping on the giant, graffitied dumpster.

Saint lets go of Allie's hand and walks to the wooden pallets, kicking them out of the way. "Finn," Saint commands, and Finn joins him. They use their legs to roll the dumpster away from them, and sitting on the ground, right where the dumpster was, is a phone.

"Found it," Cale says from beside me as we all stare at Ronan's burner phone.

7

SAINT

This is the first time that I've been to the alley. The cement is still stained with Ronan's blood, and it took all of my strength not to fall to the ground at the sight of it. The video plays in my mind, over and over. Ronan turning around, his body jerking with the force from the bullets, his body falling to the ground, and him not getting up. He died in a dirty alley, by himself. And his first thought was to call fucking Mason and ask him to cover everything up. Why didn't he call me? I would have been there before an ambulance could. Maybe I could have saved his life. I wish he were still here so I could kick his ass for that. But he's not, so what the fuck do I do with this anger? Where is it supposed to go?

Everyone thought I was grumpy before Ronan died, but since his death, all I've felt is rage. And the only place I've been able to vent it was at Allie. Now what do I do with it? I feel it bottling up inside of me. Making me explode at the slightest things, making my fingers shake, and making my stomach fill with boiling rage.

But I have to stay mad. Because if I let go of the rage, then the sadness creeps in, and that shit will fucking drown me. The overconsuming truth that the man that I looked up to for everything is fucking gone. He's gone and he's never coming back. I can never talk to him again, hear his voice, his laugh. Ask him what to do when I feel lost, or just bask in his friendship.

He's gone.

I reach down and hold Allie's hand, and she squeezes me tighter in response. I wasn't being a dick when I said she was riding with me, I did it because if she wasn't on the back of my bike, I was afraid that I'd ride into oncoming traffic just to avoid feeling this shit.

I've always gotten lost in her when things were too much, and I don't see that ever-changing. She's my peace when the feelings are raging outside.

Allie presses her cheek to my back and I take a deep breath,' letting the feel of her hands wrapped around me calm the rage that's storming inside of me.

She holds me tight the entire ride back to the clubhouse, and when she climbs off of my bike, I take her hand and pull her into my lips. "Thank you," I whisper as I pull away.

"I'm here for you. I'm *always* here for you, Saint." Her eyes hold mine, and I wish I could tell her how much I rely on her neverending strength. How thankful I am that she never gave up on us, even though I did. Maybe one day I will tell her, but right now, I can't get those words to make it out of my throat.

I nod—the only thing I *can* manage—and movement over her shoulder catches my attention. Leo steps out of the clubhouse and leans against the doorframe, watching me.

Allie turns around to follow my line of sight. Turning back around, she kisses my cheek. "Go, I'll be with Mason."

I pull her into another kiss and reluctantly let her go. I need to talk to Leo about Peyton.

Leo waits for me at the door and then follows me to the bar when I walk past him.

"How is she?" I ask, walking around the back of the bar and pulling down a bottle of Grey Goose. I fill two short tumblers with the clear alcohol and pass one to Leo.

He takes a drink and sighs after he's swallowed. "She's pretty fucked up. A few cracked ribs, broken collarbone, broken nose, sprained ankle. She's covered in bruises. They're keeping her overnight to make sure there isn't any internal bleeding."

"Fuck," I sigh. I hate that she was hurt, she's a really nice girl. She's been hanging around the clubhouse since she was fifteen. No one's ever touched her, but her mom threw her out and she didn't have anywhere to go. Ronan took her in, of course, gave her work around the clubhouse, and paid her for it. Tobi's Old Lady took her in until she was eighteen, and then she started working for Second Circle and moved in with one of the strippers. Ronan raised that girl. "Does she know who did it?"

Leo shakes his head and swallows another mouthful of vodka. "No, and she's pretty spooked. She begged me to let her stay with me when she gets out."

"Why you?" I ask, narrowing my eyes. "Were you two..." I trail off, letting him finish that sentence for me.

"Only that one time," he brushes me off. "No. She doesn't feel safe with the club. They picked her up outside of Second after her shift and dropped her off here at the gate, so she's afraid to be near the club, and my cabin's pretty remote."

I nod, thinking everything over. "Makes sense. Do you mind taking her in?" I ask, refilling my glass.

"Yeah, that's fine." He shrugs. "She's chill, and I have that extra room that I thought Jack would take, but he hasn't."

I stare at the bottle of vodka and an idea pops into my head. "Hang on, I think I have an even better idea." Pulling out my phone, I dial my favorite Russian and the man that I think I'm still in debt to.

"Mr. Viotto. I didn't think I'd be hearing from you again," Mikhail's thick Russian accent speaks down the line to me.

I watch Leo as he stares at me with his eyes narrowed in question. "I was just checking to see if you'd found a new bride yet?" I ask.

"I have not. Are you offering yours back to me?"

I clench my teeth so hard my jaw hurts, but I unlock it to answer him. "Watch your fucking mouth, Mikhail." He chuckles deeply and I contemplate hanging up. "Someone came after one of my club girls and she's pretty shaken up. I thought maybe you could get her out of town, and maybe you can win her over with your charm in the process."

He takes his sweet time answering me, which just starts to irritate me. "Has she been passed around your club?"

"No!" I snap. "But even if she has, are you really going to slut shame? How many women have you slept with?"

"That's a fair point," he relents. "Okay, I'll fly down to get her personally."

"Oh, you're not going to send someone to kidnap her from her home this time?" It comes out so fast, I don't have time to think about it and stop myself, and I slam my mouth closed once I realize what I said.

"I haven't forgotten what your club did to Vadim, Saint, I'd watch your jokes." Mikhail's voice turns dark and I internally wince.

"This isn't the same fucked up deal you had with Alexei. If Peyton wants to leave, you let her leave, or you and I will be meeting again," I say sternly. I might be a little scared of Mikhail, but he'll never know that. "You're just taking her away from Merrill Hill until she feels safe enough to return. If you happen to win her over in the meantime, great. She's a good girl and she deserves to have someone else take care of her for a change."

"Yes, why do you think I'm coming down personally? I want to make a better impression this time." I'm taken aback by how much he cares already, how eager he is to find someone, and why the fuck I have to play matchmaker for him. Why can't he meet women on his own?

"Okay. She gets out of the hospital tomorrow, so you can meet her then." I chance a look at Leo and find him staring at me with wide eyes. Yeah, this one is going to be weird to explain to everyone.

"Hospital? Is she okay?" Concern comes through clearly, and I think this might not be the worst idea I've ever had. If anyone can keep her safe and make her feel protected, it should be the head of the Bratva.

"She's pretty banged up. We don't know who came after her, but I think it might have something to do with her being connected to us," I admit, and it feels like ash on my tongue to say that. I hate that she was hurt, but I hate it more that she was hurt because of us.

"Let me know when you find them, I want their heads."

"Now you're for protecting women?" I ask, and again, it just slipped out.

"It's one of the ways I plan to win her to my side," he says, ignoring my jab.

I sigh. "Oh, Lord. Okay, Mikhail, I'll see you tomorrow." I pull the phone away from my ear and hang up.

"What. The fuck?" Leo asks as Jack sits down next to him at the bar.

"It gets Peyton out of Merrill Hill and ensures that he doesn't take an interest in my girl again. Two birds."

Leo smirks. The same smirk that gets him into any girl's

pants that he wants. "You could settle wars with your devious mind."

I shrug, walking out from behind the bar. I need to give Mason Ronan's burner to go through and I want him looking into who took Peyton. "It's just about finding out what the other person wants and working it in your favor."

8

___

SAINT

We've been in this hospital too much recently. I think I could probably walk through it with my eyes closed at this point, I feel like I know these hallways so well.

213.

212.

211. Peyton's room.

I knock on the light wood door and listen for her soft voice.

"Come in," I hear on the other side of the door.

Pushing open the door, I step through and hold in the gasp that threatens to escape my throat at the sight of Peyton sitting on the white hospital bed.

Leo said she looked bad, but fuck... Two severely black eyes, swollen and busted lips, bruises around her neck and upper arms, and a stitched cut on her temple.

"Wow, I must be special if the President himself came to break me out of here." She smirks.

"Hey, Little P." I walk to the bed and take a seat at the foot of it. "How are you doing?"

She shrugs and then winces, and I feel my heart constrict at her pain. "Better now that I've showered and changed into my own clothes. I can't wait to go to Leo's cabin." She sighs with such relief that I feel bad about what I'm about to tell her, but it's for the best—for her and Allie.

"Actually, I arranged something else for you," I say slowly.

Her swollen eyes narrow as best they can. "What do you mean?"

My phone vibrates and I pull it out of my jeans, thankful for the momentary distraction. I should have sent Finn to do this. If she doesn't want to go, I'm going to have a hard time not forcing her to go.

It's a video from Mason, which is odd. He always calls or texts me; he never sends me videos. I'll open it after this.

Coughing, I clear my throat and focus back on Peyton. Fuck, she looks really bad. "Leo said that you were afraid to be alone and be at the clubhouse. I have a friend in New York that said you could stay with him until you feel comfortable enough to come back." I watch her closely.

"What about my job?" Peyton asks, settling against the pillow behind her.

"It will be here whenever you come back, and my friend said you don't have to worry about anything while you're there," I assure her.

She shakes her head lightly, her pink hair falling limp around her slim shoulders. "I can't just live off of this person, I don't even know who... Wait..." Her face scrunches up, her eyes narrowing again. "Are you selling me off to man!?" Her voice raises and my face falls. I'm almost offended she would think that of me.

"I'd never do that to you, P. He is hoping to win you over, but I made it clear that if you wanted to come home, we were coming to get you. The club has always looked out for you. This gets you safely out of Washington." I level with her. No matter how you cut it, this is a good plan. She gets to live the good life in New York with no expectations.

"Is he an Outlaw?" she asks, her tempter settling.

I shake my head, not wanting to tell her who Mikhail is, but I've been honest this far, so I might as well continue. "No, he's the head of the New York Bratva."

"Oh, fuck," she groans, resting her head on the pillow.

Standing up, I offer her my hand. "Come on, I'll wheel you down to meet lover boy." Peyton's laugh feels like a weight lifting off of my shoulders. I am doing this for partly selfish reasons, but I do care about Peyton and I think this will be good for her. If anyone could handle someone like Peyton, it would be a mafia boss. She's a lot.

"Are you sure about this, Saint?" Peyton asks quietly, standing in front of me.

I nod, "Yeah, P. I wouldn't send you if I didn't think you'd be safe."

She squeezes my hand and lets go. "Okay, I'll get my bag."

Ding.

The elevator chimes as the door opens, and Peyton releases a shaky breath. "Here we go," she says.

I push her forward, into the hallway that leads to the waiting room. "If you don't want to go, just say the word and we'll go out the back."

"No." She shakes her head. "I want to go. I need to get out of here for a while."

I stop the wheelchair and look down at her. "We're going to find who attacked you, P."

She turns around in the chair and winces, so I walk around to her front, kneeling down. "Be careful, Saint. I remember them talking before I passed out. They're going to come after the club."

My blood starts pumping faster, but I hold my face still. "Who, Peyton?"

She shakes her head and wets her lips. "I don't know for sure. I never saw their faces."

I nod once and stand, rounding the back of her wheelchair. "Okay. Let's get you out of here then."

The waiting room is empty, except for Mikhail and two of his men. He stands with his side facing us, one hand in the pocket of his brown slacks, with the other holding a large bouquet. Oh hell, Peyton's going to run right over him. Tattoos trail out of the rolled-up sleeves of his white shirt.

He glances sideways at us as we approach. "Wow," he breathes as he turns to face us.

"Yeah, I know. I look like two assholes beat the shit out of me." Peyton cocks her head. "Oh, wait," she snarks.

I raptly watch the conversation. "No. You're beautiful, and I will bring you the heads of everyone who touched you. I promise, malen'kaya kukla." He stands over her and takes his hand out of his pocket, offering it to her.

She stares at his hand, his gold pinky ring glinting under the harsh lights in the waiting room.

Finally, she takes it and he helps her up, but she immediately drops his hand once she is standing.

He holds the bouquet out to her and she swats them away. "I'm not giving birth or dying. Throw those away before I lay them on your grave."

Mikhail chuckles under his breath and smirks, holding the flowers up for one of his goons to take from him. "I'm Mikhail Belov." He offers Peyton his hand to shake.

She takes it and I watch him stare at their joined hands. He's really taking this seriously. "Yeah, I know. Big mafia boss." She holds his eyes, even though she's half his size.

He casts an unamused glance at me, which I return with a

shrug. Like I wasn't going to tell her. "I wouldn't go around announcing that, Peyton." My eyes narrow. This motherfucker looked her up...or pulled her file from the nurse's station.

"So, New York?" she asks. "Do we have a flight to get to?"

He smiles warmly at her, no trace of the ice he was sending my way. "My plane takes off when you're ready. We'll be in New York for a few days and then we're going to Russia for a while."

"I don't have a passport." Peyton looks away.

Mikhail shakes his head, waving away her concern. "I'll take care of it, malen'kaya kukla."

Her eyes soften as she looks at him, and I get the feeling that she won't be coming home. I step up and break their trance with each other. "I'll see you around, Little P." I open my arms for her to hug me. She's the only girl outside of my family and Allie that I let hug me. I take her in my arms and lean down to whisper in her ear. "One call and we'll be on the first flight to come get you, no matter where you are."

"I know," she whispers back before pulling away.

Mikhail takes Peyton's small bag from me and I watch them walk out of the hospital and to a waiting car, with his men trailing behind them. I know I'm doing the right thing, but it doesn't mean that it's exactly easy to see Peyton go. She's been hanging out with the club for seven years, longer than I've even been a member. I know she'll be okay.

When their car pulls away, I walk out to my bike, straddling it, when I remember the video Mason sent a while ago.

I open my phone and pull up his messages. The video starts and it's Allie standing in front of the camera.

"What are you waiting for, Solnyshko?" Mason asks and Allie leans forward with lust shining in her eyes as she stares up at Mason. I click on his number, dialing him before I can watch my girl put his dick in her mouth.

"Took you long enough," Mason breathes heavily. "Are you

on your way to Allie's yet? She's still wet enough for you." Allie's squeals in the background turn into a moan and I hang up on a chuckling Mason.

Motherfucker.

9

ALLIE

I wake in my bed alone, and stretch my legs and arms wide. I wouldn't trade sleeping with both of my men for anything, but it is kind of nice to be able to lay in the middle of the bed, not squished between two rock hard bodies, for just a moment.

As I'm starfished out in the middle of the bed, soaking up the silence, the sound of my bedroom door opening draws my attention.

Mason walks inside, holding onto the top of the towel that's wrapped around his waist. Small water droplets are sparsely dotted over his tan shoulders, a few starting to drip down his chiseled chest.

"Did Saint leave for the hospital?" I ask. He had mentioned it last night, but I thought he would have woken us to go with him.

Mason nods, closing the door behind him. "Yeah, he didn't want to wake you."

Rolling over, I grab a pillow and tuck it between my cheek and arm. "I feel like I haven't had much time with you since the whole video thing."

"I'm here now, and it's just the two of us." He smirks, his sea-green eyes sparkling.

Sitting up slowly, I let the thin strap of my silk sleep top slip over my shoulder. "That is true. We could talk, or have a cup of coffee." I bite my lip, holding back a smile.

Mason shakes his head slowly, his smirk growing in size. "I have a much better idea of what you can do with your mouth."

"Is that so?" I cock my head to the side and take the second strap between my fingers, slowly moving it down my arm.

Mason's eyes trace the movement. "Yeah, but I want to see something first."

"What's that?" I ask.

His eyes finally return to mine. "I want you to crawl to me." His voice turns to a lustful rasp.

With locked eyes, I push the comforter over my bent knees and step out of my bed. I sink to my hands and knees on the plush carpet and slowly crawl to Mason.

He widens his stance, dropping the towel at his feet as I move across the floor.

Using that gesture as my invitation, I run my hands up his strong legs, stopping at his hips. His cock stands erect in my face.

"Wait, I want to record this." He walks around me and grabs his phone from the bedside table. After returning to me, he aims the camera at my face and smirks. "What are you waiting for, Solnyshko?" he asks, looking at me with half-lidded eyes.

I take him into my mouth, too eager to go slow. I take him down as deep as I can, with my hands gripping his waist.

His head falls back as he sighs out his pleasure, and my eyes bounce from the camera to him. I don't know where to look, but the thought of Mason watching this later is a huge turn on. I want to perform for him. I want him to watch this and remember how great I felt wrapped around him.

These thoughts spur me on and I put everything I have into sucking him. I flick my tongue, swivel my hand, and cup his balls. I want to blow his mind.

"Okay, okay, okay," Mason sighs, moving away. "I need your pussy, Solnyshko. I need more of you. Bend over the bed and arch that back for me," Mason demands. Rising to my feet, I turn around and bend over the foot of my bed, laying my arms out flat and arching my back so my ass is raised in the air. "Yeah, just like that, good girl. Is this pussy ready for me?" he asks.

"Yes," I moan as two fingers trace from my clit to my leaking pussy.

Mason rubs the head of his cock around in my wetness before slowly pushing inside of me.

We moan in unison as he seats himself deep inside of me. Turning to look over my shoulder, I see Mason still recording us, the phone pointed right at where we're joined. I arch my back more, and mason starts fucking me faster, slaps of skin and moans filling the room.

"Fuck, Allie. You always feel so good," Mason groans, one hand sliding up my back and anchoring to my shoulder so he can thrust harder.

"Yes. harder," I moan, pressing my cheek into the bed and savoring every amazing push of his cock inside of me.

Sex has never been this great. My men know everywhere to stroke, to touch, to kiss, and to suck. They know my body and what I need, and they never fail to deliver exactly what I ask for.

Mason's short and hard thrusts push me over the edge, and I bury my face into the comforter as I moan through my orgasm.

Mason slows his hips, coaxing me back to Earth. "Do you want both of us, baby?" he asks. "Me and Sainty fucking you at the same time, filling both holes?" He pulls almost completely out and then slowly slides back inside. I whimper at the thought of both of them at the same time. The thought alone almost pushes me over the edge again. Mason pulls out and replaces his dick with his fingers, continuing the slow pumping. "Oh, yeah you do, baby, the thought of fucking us both made you drenched." He pushes all the way inside of me and leans over me. "But you're never going to forget who fucks this pussy the best are you?" he whispers into my ear.

"Mason," I moan. Though, I honestly can't choose who is better between them. They both blow my mind every single time.

He chuckles deeply and rises again, grabbing onto my hips with both hands. "That's what I thought," he says arrogantly. I lift my head and see the camera pointing right at my face on the bed, propped against a pillow.

I let every thrust show on my face as Mason fucks me at a fast pace into the bed. I'm not exaggerating anything, but I am making sure he sees how much I'm enjoying myself.

A second orgasm builds quickly and it hits me like a wave: hard and never ending.

Mason grunts behind me, and when he's spent himself inside of me, he collapses next to me on the bed.

As his chest heaves, he reaches for his phone.

"What are you doing?" I ask, rolling over and setting my head on Mason's sweaty chest. I don't care. I love being close to my men, especially after an orgasm.

"I took two videos and I sent the first one to Saint," he chuckles.

"No you didn't!" I exhale loudly, my chest rising and falling quickly with my short breaths. Saint's going to lose his mind.

Mason licks his lips and my pussy flutters with post-orgasm aftershocks at the devilish look on his face. "I'm just trying to figure out if he's really all in." Mason presses a kiss to my temple.

"Don't push him. He'll come when he's ready," I chastise Mason.

"He'll cum today," he says. "In here, where I did." He pushes two fingers into my soaking pussy.

"Oh, fuck," I moan, rolling further into Mase's side.

Mason strokes inside of me slowly. "He's here," he states, and pulls his fingers out.

"What?" I ask, dazed, right before I hear my front door slam closed. Oh, shit.

Saint storms into my bedroom, my door bouncing off the wall as he enters. "Get out!" he barks, hooking his thumb over his shoulder.

"Oh, come on, I got her warmed up for you. The least you could do is let me watch," Mason bargains.

"Out!" Saint shouts louder.

Mason rolls his eyes with a smile on his lips as he slides off of the bed and picks his boxers up off of the floor and pulls them over his strong, tan thighs. He stands, smiling so brightly, and my chest constricts. I love him so much it hurts.

I love them both so much that it hurts.

Whether we're hurting each other or ourselves, I'll love them until my last breath, of that I'm sure.

Mason strides to the nightstand and picks up his phone. "Time" by NF starts to play from the small bluetooth speaker on my vanity.

He turns around with his phone and walks to the door where Saint is still standing, glaring at Mason the entire way. "Gotta try to drown out her moans, or else I won't be able to stop myself from coming back in." He chuckles as he brushes past Saint and into the hallway.

Saint slams the door closed, his eyes pinned on my naked body splayed across my bed. He pulls at his clothes as he stomps to me, ripping them off of his body like an animal with no control.

I can't take my eyes off of him, his muscles rippling with his movements, until he stands bare before me at the edge of the bed.

"You're a brat for that stunt." He glares at me, but his cock juts from his body, telling me he didn't mind it too much.

"I didn't do it," I say sweetly, raising my eyes to his.

"You're both brats," he breaths, lowering himself onto the bed and crawling over my body. "Brats who should be punished instead of rewarded," he says next to my ear, his warm breath washing over my neck and rising goosebumps.

"If you deny me, you'll also be denying yourself, and where's the fun in that?" I turn my head and nip at his shoulder. A proud smile pulls at my lips as his entire body shudders above me.

"I'm done denying my Queen." His open palm slowly slides down the side of my body, tracing my curves with his strong hand. "How many times did he make you cum?" his husky voice asks.

I arch my back, pressing my aching nipples into his hot chest. "Twice," I answer.

"Fucking amateur." Saint grunts as his hand cups my pussy. He slides a finger inside of me, massaging. "Are you wet for me or him?" he asks.

I pull away so I can turn my head to look into his ice-blue eyes. "Both of you," I answer honestly.

Saint watches me for a moment before I see him swallow, his Adam's apple bobbing in his throat. "I can work with that."

A shuddering breath escapes from my throat, and I feel so overwhelmed that I want to cry. The weeks that he pushed me away for loving them both are fresh on my mind, and I feel like if we push him too far, he'll leave and hate me again.

But this confirmation means the world to me. All I've ever wanted was to love someone more than I love myself; to feel the overbearing feeling that I couldn't live without someone, and when I felt that for two men, I couldn't comprehend it. How could I feel so deeply for two men at the same time?

You're only supposed to have one soulmate, and I have two.

The realization that I just might be able to have both of them? I've never been happier.

"Fuck me, Saint," I whisper. "Like you hate me," I add on with a smirk.

He laughs above me and reaches down to align his cock. "Anything for you, my Queen."

He presses the tip of his cock into me, and I toss my head back in ecstasy, moaning.

"You're mine, Allie," Saint growls before he flattens his tongue and runs it up the column of my neck.

THUMP! THUMP! THUMP! "Saint, we gotta go!" Mason yells from the other side of the door.

"Fuck off!" Saint bellows from above me, his arms straining deliciously as he holds himself up.

"I found something on Ro's burner, and we gotta get to the clubhouse!

Saint groans before releasing a harsh breath. "Go," I encourage. "The sooner we take care of this, the sooner I have you both back."

"Fuck." Saint sighs, pulling out and kneeling before me. The head of his cock is slick and glistening. "I'm coming back for this." He slides two fingers inside of me, collecting my wetness to rub over my clit.

I raise my hips to follow his finger, but he pulls it away with a glare.

He climbs off the bed and redresses, then walks into my closet. I hear drawers opening and closing as I roll over and peer in after him.

"You still have this?" Saint says from inside my closet.

"Still have what?" I ask, propping myself up on my elbow. He walks to the door and holds up his long sleeve shirt that I wore home from his house. "I wear it to sleep in sometimes," I admit quietly.

He walks over and sets the clothes on the bed next to me, his eyes roaming over my naked body while he slowly lays the clothes down.

"What's that for?" I ask.

"I don't want you alone until we know what's going on." I roll my eyes, and Saint's narrow at me. "Allie, I don't even know who to protect you from right now, so please just get dressed and come with us."

"Fine." I sit up and look over the clothes he picked out again. His shirt with a pair of distressed denim shorts. "You forgot my panties." I raise one brow at him.

Saint shakes his head, a small smile pulling at his lips. "No, I didn't." With that, he turns and walks to the door. Fuck that, I'm grabbing underwear before we leave.

Saint opens it quickly and on the other side is a smirking Mason. "Watch your back, Underwood," Saint snaps as he steps around a chuckling Mason.

10

SAINT

"You know that you're truly happy when you stop looking for tricks and thrills and start to enjoy the mundane." That's what Ronan had told me once, and I didn't understand why he would say that when he was still chasing thrills and fucking club whores. But as I ride with Allie's arms wrapped around me, Mason at our side, "Double Take" by dhruv playing through Mason's speakers, and the warm Washington air blowing past us as we ride through town, I finally get it.

I'm content in my life. Or, at least, I would be, if we weren't chasing half-clues and mysteries. But this. Our girl with us. This is true happiness.

Mason called the rest of the club, and they're all waiting for us when we step into the clubhouse. Finn, Cale, Nate, Tobi, Wyatt, Leo, and Jack are spread out and sitting around the front room, talking to each other and laughing. I have no idea if we're about to ruin their moods, but I'm sure we are. When aren't we getting bad fucking news?

"Chapel, guys," I say, gesturing toward the room.

Allie pulls my arm back, and I turn around to look at her.

Mason stops and waits with me. "Soph is calling, so I'm going to stay out here and talk to her." She holds up her phone.

"Okay." I nod. Thank fuck for that. I was about to tell her she wasn't allowed in Church and I was not wanting to put up with that fight again.

Mason and I watch her walk to the bar and sit down before we turn and walk to the Chapel together. Shoulder to shoulder, like fucking pals.

God, sharing a girl with a brother in a more intimate way than just sex? What the fuck have I gotten myself into?

She's worth it, though.

"Alright, first, Peyton was released from the hospital this morning. She's doing alright. She's pretty bruised up, but she hasn't lost any of her grit, so I know she'll be okay eventually," I say, settling into my chair at the head of the table.

"That's great," Tobi's deep voice cuts through the silence.

"I was really worried about her," Nate admits.

I bite my lip. There's definitely going to push back on this. "I was too. She's really shaken though, so I sent her to stay with a friend in New York."

"Who, Prez?" Finn asks, his eyes narrowing on me. He has an idea of where this is going, I can already tell.

"Mikhail Belov." No sense in beating around the bush, right?

"What?" Cale cocks his head to the side, pieces of blonde hair falling into his eyes.

Tobi grunts, "Absolutely not!" He booms down the table. "Outlaws take care of family!"

I turn my icy glare to him. The old bat is always protesting like he runs this damn place, but would never actually take up the gavel. "We are taking care of family! She didn't want to be anywhere near anything Outlaw. She's terrified to be associated with us right now, so being in New York with Mikhail gets her away from us and out of town." I shake my head, a quiet chuckle falling out. "And do you really think Peyton couldn't handle herself? I made it clear to Mikhail that when she's ready to come home, he's putting her on the first flight." Looking away from Tobi, so he knows that I'm done with that, I face Mason. "So, what did you find?" I ask Mason, who sits on the other side of Cale.

Mason slides Ronan's burner to me across the table. "Ronan was supposed to be meeting someone in that alley."

"Who?" Finn asks, his fingers flicking his lighter around in a circle on the table.

Mason shrugs. "I'm not sure. He was messaging with a burner that I can't trace."

"Was he meeting with Joseph?" I ask, scrolling through the texts.

"Maybe." Mason bites his lip. "I really don't know. I just know that Ronan was going to meet someone because they said they had information that Los Lobos were the ones who killed Michelle Davis and were framing us."

I keep my eyes on Mason. I think I can trust him. I know that he didn't kill Ronan. I can see it in his eyes. "Did Joseph's phone ping anywhere near where Ro was killed?"

Mason shakes his head. "No, but if they planned to frame me for his murder from the beginning, then it would make sense that they would know not to have his phone in the area." He's got a point.

"No matter how many times we analyze this, or how many different ways we look at it, it all comes down to one thing." I pause, looking around at my brothers sitting at the table around me. My family. "Los Lobos killed our President and then tried to frame Mason. I'm not letting that stand."

"Hell fucking no!" Tobi shouts from down the table.

"What do you want to do, Prez?" Nate asks.

I sigh, thinking. Should I make this call? Is this what Ronan would do? He would do this if it were me. "Outlaws don't take cheap shots. We don't let things slide, and when we strike, we hit back just as hard." My brothers watch me, every single one watching me for guidance. For my decision. "Ronan wouldn't let it stand if he lost any of you." I've made up my mind. "President for President. We take out their leader."

We're going to war.

11

MASON

OH MY GOD…

I've never regretted my decision to join the Outlaws. Not when I had to clean bathrooms after a party, or when I had to sit outside of Reese's apartment for hours, and my ass would fall asleep and my eyes would cross from lack of sleep. Not when I had to clean the viruses from Nate's computer because he can't stop clicking on sketchy porn sites, and then I accidentally stumbled across his dick pics.

I stubbornly wanted to fuck over the government, and I thought joining a club would get me in touch with some shady people, which it definitely did.

I didn't regret it when I killed Vadim, because he was coming after Allie. But to go after a gang and start a war with them makes me second guess my choices up until now.

All of them but one.

Allie.

And then I feel guilt over my questioning, because my brother died. One of the first people to show me kindness in this world. The first person to show me what it meant for someone to have my back, no matter what happened; to trust me with his life, and to promise to protect me with it. I just don't want anything to blow back on Allie or the other girls.

That would be the logical place to hit an organization, right? Their women?

I'm scared.

For the first time in my life, I have something that I'm scared to death to lose.

I love Allie more than I want revenge, and I feel like such a piece of shit for saying that about Ronan, because I know he would avenge me.

So I sit quietly, because the vibrating rage that is pouring off of Saint, Nate, and Tobi is terrifying. The arrogance that radiates out of Leo is alarming. The haunted look on Cale and Finn's faces is telling. And the sheer calm that is always present with Jack is unsettling. The tired wear on Wyatt's features worries me. He's done with the club—or life in general, I don't know. But I know I need to check on him.

But no one looks unsure.

We're doing this, whether we think this is the right choice or not. We follow our President to hell and back, because we trust that he has the club's best interest at heart.

I just pray that Saint's decision isn't shadowed by grief and anger.

He will not survive if something happens to Allie. It would kill him from the inside to lose Allie and Ronan to this, but it wouldn't kill him before I did.

So I will trust him, but I will always put my girl first.

Our girl.

Everyone leaves the Chapel in a somber mood, and Finn and Cale leave the clubhouse completely.

The guys mingle around the bar, not really sure what to do, but I know exactly where I need to go. Saint and I need to tell Allie what's about to happen.

"Why are you leaving now, what's going on?" Allie shakes her head, looking up at Saint as he wraps her in his arms.

"We have to go now, Allie. We can't wait for them to plan another attack," he says calmly into her hair.

Her jaw is set, and I can tell she doesn't like this at all. I don't blame her. Saint lets go of her and steps aside. She crashes into my chest and I hold onto her like it'll be my last time, just in case it is. "I don't like this, Mase," she whispers into my chest.

"I know, Solnyshko, but we'll be back. I'm coming back for you," I say, steeling my voice and looking to Saint for strength. She won't tell him that she's scared, that she doesn't like our plan. She knows he won't understand like I do. He was too close to Ronan. "I'll keep his head clear," I whisper against her lips before kissing her.

I let her go, even though it's the last thing I want to do, and she grabs hold of Saint's arm, her nails digging into his skin.

"Look after each other." Her wide eyes swing between us. "I need you both to come back, so protect each other, or I will come in there and get you."

"I promise, my Queen," Saint says, and I nod because I don't trust myself to not say I'm not going. But she's right. I need to make sure Saint doesn't get himself killed because he's unfocused.

———

FINN AND CALE pull in through the compound gates in two black SUVs, and I watch as Wyatt leads Reese into the clubhouse. Brothers walk past me, carrying rifles to the SUVs as others load a few crates of bullets. Club girls hurry into the clubhouse and Nate and Tobi walk the fence. And I stand in the middle of the asphalt, watching everyone.

Leo steps out of his Mustang that he drove in a few moments ago.

"All good?" Saint asks, walking up beside me.

"All good." Leo smirks.

Saint shakes his head, scratching at his blond beard. "Do I want to know what you had to do to get it?"

Leo rolls his eyes, his tongue darting out to wet his lips. "What I'm best at. She wanted two Outlaws, but Jack wouldn't do it and I can't share with Mason anymore." His eyes slide to mine and I bite the inside of my cheek. It was one time.

"What about Nate, Tobi, or Wyatt?" Saint asks, chuckling roughly.

Leo scoffs. "Wyatt maybe, but I'm not slapping my balls with Nate and Tobi's wrinkly ones." His face scrunches up and I choke on my laugh.

"They're the same age!" I interject.

Leo waves me off. "She confirmed that Miguel will be at Sammy's Bar. She said she can get him outside for 10K."

Saint nods. "Tell her if she gets him outside at your call, the money is hers, but I'm not protecting her if she gets caught."

"I'll call her now." Leo takes his phone out.

"You had to fuck her *and* pay her?" I ask, a laugh in my voice.

Leo shrugs, raising his phone to his ear. "The sex was for the information, the money is for helping us—or getting out of town —I don't know—" He cuts off his sentence quickly. "Hey, baby, miss me?" He walks away while I shake my head.

"Packed and ready to go!" Finn shouts.

Saint walks away without a word to me, and I follow after him.

Tobi slides into the driver's seat of one of the SUVs, with Nate in the passenger side. Jack gets into the back, with an AR strapped to his chest, and Leo gets in across from him, still on his phone.

I stand and watch as Finn gets into the other SUV with Cale beside him and Saint getting into the back. I guess that's where I'm going.

I open the backseat door and see Saint slipping rounds into a magazine. I slam the door behind me as Saint slots the magazine in the AR with a loud click.

I release a deep breath and watch the clubhouse as we pull out of the parking lot.

Here we go.

Finn relays the plan to the guys in the car behind us as he drives, and Leo confirms that the girl he met with—a bartender at Sammy's—will get Miguel outside somehow at our signal.

The car ride is silent and tense. No one speaks, and the only sounds are our breathing and the ticking blinker. I've never known a time when Finn and Cale weren't shooting the shit, or pestering Saint, and it just shows how serious this is.

This will start a war.

One that Saint is confident we will win, but aren't those the ones you usually lose?

I still don't know if this is the right choice.

Sammy's bar comes into view way too quickly, and we stop down the road, waiting for Leo to signal the girl.

We watch the dark parking lot outside of the rundown bar with baited breath, and still, no one speaks.

I take out my phone and text Allie.

MASON:

I love you.

I watch my phone for when she opens it, but it stays unopened. I guess I should expect that. She's with Reese and Huntley, and they're probably consumed in something, but I kind of hoped that she'd be waiting by her phone with worry.

"There!" Cale's sharp voice cuts through my thoughts and I slip my phone back in my pocket.

Finn turns around and I follow his sight to Saint, moving to face the window and settling the gun against his shoulder. "For Ronan," he says, gritting his teeth.

"For Ronan," Finn echos, turning around and gunning the gas.

Cale rolls down Saint's window from the front seat, and I turn to watch everything. If I'm going to do this, I'm going to be all in.

We speed into the parking lot, with the second SUV right behind us, Jack hanging out of the window with his gun aimed.

Miguel stands at the front, wiping at his shirt with a napkin. He barely has time to look up before Saint pops off three rounds. Two in his chest, one in his head, and he falls to the ground. Finn stomps on the gas, but someone sprints around the corner of the bar with a gun raised. Saint is still looking out the window, savoring his revenge, and not watching.

I yank him back by the back of his shirt, both of us falling on the cream leather seats while a bullet flies above us and pierces the window on my side.

"Oh, fuck!" Cale ducks in the front seat, his arm swinging out and landing on Finn's thick bicep.

Another few shots ring out as Finn picks up speed. "Jack got him," he says as he takes a turn way too fast.

Saint and I sit up, and he stares at me. "Thanks," he says quietly.

"You would have done the same thing for me." I brush him off. He probably would have died if I hadn't grabbed him, but I don't want this to feel like a big deal.

"Not a few weeks ago, I wouldn't have," he admits. "Or at least I would have thought about not doing it." He sets the AR on the floor and rolls the window up.

The walkie talkie that we were using to talk to everyone in the other SUV scratches before Nate's voice comes down the line. "Everyone good?" he asks.

Saint reaches forward and takes the walkie from Finn. "All good, he missed. You all good?"

"We're good," Nate answers. "Jack got the bastard that took the shot at you."

Saint sighs and rests his head against the backrest. A few pieces of long blond hair fall into his face. "Are they going to know it was us?" I ask, looking around the car at my brothers.

"Probably. I carved Ronan's name into the bullets," Saints says, his eyes closed as he rests against the seat.

12

ALLIE

"So you actually made it happen? Saint and Mason? Wow."
Reese shakes her head, chuckling under her breath.

I bite my lip to hold in my smile. "Well, you did tell me not to settle, so I got two loves instead of one."

Reese barks out a laugh. "It's not what I had in mind when I said that, but as long as you're happy, then I'm happy."

"I love you so much, Reese." I reach across the bar and take her delicate hands.

She smiles, leaning closer to me. "I love you too, Al."

My phone vibrates on the bartop and I pick it up, hoping for a message from Saint or Mason to tell me they're on their way back to the clubhouse. But instead, it's an alert from the security system Mase installed.

I click on the app and a video pops up, showing Soph trying to get into the house. I exit out of the app quickly and raise my phone to call her. I completely forgot to tell her about the new alarm and passcode.

Rising from the bar, I motion to my phone for Reese and then walk towards the door. It's loud in here with all of the club girls, Nox, Wyatt, and Huntley.

"What the fuck?" Sophie yells over the blaring alarm on the other end of the phone.

"About that, we have a security system." I hold in my laughter, walking into the parking lot, aimlessly.

"Is this your way of kicking me out?" Sophie scolds, but I can hear a slight laugh in her voice. "Oh my God," she groans. "The neighbors are coming out to stare at me."

I lose in my battle to contain my laugh, and let out a loud chuckle. "The passcode is 2384. I'm sorry for forgetting to tell you about it."

I hear the beeping of the buttons and the alarm cutting off. "That was so embarrassing," Soph hisses, but someone standing on the other side of the road catches my attention. I hang up on Sophie, barely hearing her goodbye.

He's staring at the gate...or at me.

He's wearing a ski mask and he slowly cocks his head as he stares at me.

I quickly turn around—I have to tell Wyatt and Nox that he's here—but I slam into a hard body.

"Nox—" I trail off when I look up and realize that I didn't run into one of our guys, but another tall man in a ski mask.

This guy isn't an Outlaw.

"The President's girl. I've been looking for you." His macabre smile is the last thing that I see as he stabs me in the neck with a needle.

13

SAINT

EVERYONE WHO STAYED AT THE CLUBHOUSE IS OUTSIDE WHEN WE pull back through the gates. Wide eyes and pursed lips greet us, and when I get out of the SUV, I look around at everyone.

I don't see her.

An uneasy chill slides up my spine at the familiar feeling of looking for someone in this parking lot and not finding them.

Wyatt walks up to me, and Mason lingers slightly behind me. My fingers clutch the collar of Wyatt's shirt and I yank him toward me. "Where is Allie?" He opens his mouth, but his eyes are already telling me that I'm about to fucking kill him. "Where the fuck is she!?" I shout at him, and I barely see some of the club girls flinch in response.

Reese pushes around Callum and touches my outstretched arm that's still holding onto Wyatt. "She stepped out of the club-house to call Sophie, and she never came back inside."

Mason stalks around me, his stride measured and angry. His shoes punch the pavement with every step towards the clubhouse.

My hand unwraps from Wyatt's shirt, and I stare down at it. It's shaking.

No.

I'm trembling. Every muscle in my body is tightened, and my breathing quickens. In my mind, I can see the alley where Ronan died, but instead of Ronan bleeding out on the pavement, I see Allie.

My mind breaks.

Every muscle in my body stops working, and I fall to my knees. I don't even feel the crushing pain of smacking my knees on the concrete. Someone took her. She's in danger. Or worse.

Finn heaves my body up from the ground and wraps an arm around me. "We're going to find her, Saint," his raspy voice speaks into my ear.

I shake my head, every sensation leaving my body besides an empty cold, like the chill that rushes through your veins when you get an IV. "We didn't find Ronan in time," I say.

Finn ushers me toward the clubhouse. "We have a head start this time."

We pass people and some follow us, but I don't pay them any attention. They're just blurs as we walk. "He called Mason after he was shot. We could have saved him." The surveillance video plays on a loop in my head. Honestly, it has been doing that ever since I saw it. But now, the thought of Allie being in a video like that is crippling.

"He won't let that happen again," Finn speaks with such strength—such conviction—I believe him. I have to. Mason loves Allie, and I know he will do everything he can to find her before anything happens to her.

But what if we're already too late?

When we step inside the clubhouse, Huntley's sharp eyes fall on us and she joins us, holding onto me from the opposite side of Finn. She quietly accompanies us up the stairs and into Mason's room. I appreciate that she doesn't say anything.

Mason is typing furiously on his computer and I see a globe spinning on one of his monitors.

"I'm tracking her phone now, and checking the cameras in the lot." A ping interrupts him and the globe zooms in quickly before it shows an aerial view of the compound. "Her phone is still here," he says, switching to the cameras.

"Where? I'll go look." The fog surrounding my mind clears and I feel the first deadly pang of hope creeping through my veins, but that's not something I can afford to have right now. Because if I have hope and I lose her... I'm following her into the grave. I've already come to that conclusion.

"By the gate," Mason says. I leave Finn's side and hurry for the door. "Saint..." Mason leaves the sentence hanging in the air, and I know what he's thinking.

"I know she's not here, she would be with us if she were," I say over my shoulder and leave without another word.

The commotion in the parking lot has moved into the club-house, and every eye follows me as I walk through to the door. I know they're watching me to see what I do, how I handle this. Can they see the cracks? Can they see how close I am to losing my mind?

Birds squawk as they fly from one towering tree to the next, and I walk across the deserted parking lot. My mind is racing, my thoughts jumbling together. What was the last thing I said to her? I kissed her before I left, right? Could this be retaliation for Miguel? Logically, I know that this isn't because of Miguel—the hit *just* happened. There wasn't enough time for them to rally together and plan a kidnapping.

I still find myself wondering if I'm the reason Allie was taken.

Of course I'm the reason. No one is safe with the Outlaws anymore.

Things have changed—shifted. We went from the hunters to the hunted, and I wonder how long the rest of us have left.

I know one thing for sure, though. We will fight until our last breath.

My feet stop in their tracks when I see Allie's phone laying on the concrete. Bending down, I pick it up and swipe it unlocked after entering her passcode. I might have watched over her shoulder one night; we can't all be hacker geniuses. Her phone is still on her call log, her last outgoing call was to Sophie. She has an unread text from Mason.

I knew her phone was abandoned in the parking lot. I knew she wouldn't be with it, but it still feels like a sucker punch to the gut to see it laying on the ground and her nowhere in sight. Allie doesn't go anywhere without her phone, and we lost the one way we could track her. I should have chipped her when she was passed out in my bed.

Her phone thunks onto Mase's desk as I drop it beside him.

"Recognize him?" Mason asks, pointing to the screen to the side of him while he switches between camera feeds on the screen in front of him.

Stepping around him, I lean down beside him and look at the screen grab that's pulled up on the wide screen. A man stands with his back to the camera, walking up to Allie as she stares at the compound gate and hangs up her phone. He's wearing a black hoodie with the hood pulled up, average height, average weight. Every inch of him is covered. There isn't any way to tell who he is.

"Is that a trick question?" I ask, staring at the screen harder.

"Just a hopeful question." Mason continues to watch his screen as his cursor moves onto my screen and presses play.

I grip the edge of the desk, my knuckles turning white as I watch the piece of shit plunge a needle into Allie's neck and watch as she falls to the ground, unconscious.

"Fucking find her, Mason," I seethe, watching the man scoop Allie up and carry her to the gate, where he cut a hole in the fence. He steps through it and tosses her limp body into the backseat of a pickup that drove up.

"I'm fucking trying!" Mason shouts next to me. The sound doesn't even register with me, because I can't take my eyes off of the now-empty camera feed. We have to find her. "They put her in a helicopter," Mason says slowly, his eyes narrowing on the traffic cam footage he's watching. He tracked them through various cameras, following the pickup as it went through town.

"How long ago?" I ask, watching the screen as the helicopter's propellers turn on and the aircraft lifts from the ground.

"An hour ago. Fuck," Mason sighs.

Dragging my hand down my face, I drop to my ass and sit on the floor next to Mason's chair. An hour already? They could be anywhere by now. Hundreds of miles away.

Minutes pass, feeling like hours, and with every passing second, I feel myself fall deeper and deeper into a pit of darkness. Emotions seep out of me until there isn't anything left. I will not live without Allie.

"The last GPS coordinate of the helicopter is a small island in the Sound," Mason breaks the heavy silence.

"What?" I ask, staring up at Mase as he pushes his chair out and stands.

"Let's go," he urges impatiently.

"What are we doing?" I hate that he's the one having to take charge right now—that he's the one leading me, instead of the other way around. I always keep my cool.

"I think Miles can get us a helicopter. If not, then we're stealing one. Do you have to hotwire a helicopter?" He walks out of the door and I scramble to my feet to follow him.

14

MASON

"I'M GETTING REALLY FUCKING TIRED OF SEEING YOUR UGLY FACE IN my camera," Miles sighs.

Saint pushes me aside. "Our girl is missing and I need a helicopter. Let me in or I'm jumping this fucking gate."

"Oh, joy. You brought grumpy," Miles says as the gate starts to roll away.

By the time we get through the second gate and to the house, Miles is standing on his front porch with his arms crossed. "Where are we going?"

"You're coming?" Saint asks, stepping up to the porch.

Miles looks between us with a bored look. "Do any of you know how to fly a helicopter?" Saint and I look at each other and then back at Leo and Jack—we all shake our heads. "Let's go get your girl, then."

He takes off around the side of his house and into the woods, and we follow closely behind him.

I never knew that Miles had a helicopter and a landing pad in his forest of fuckery. I knew he could fly and that he has crazy connections, but I didn't know he owned one in his backyard!

I climb into the second seat while Saint, Jack, and Leo slide into the back, and I give my phone to Miles, showing the island that we need to land on. Every passing minute that Allie isn't with us is detrimental. I'm terrified for her, but I can see Saint breaking down, so I'm trying to be strong for all of us. Because that's the only way this fucked up three way will work: we have to work as one. We can't be selfish.

Miles squints at my phone and then zooms out and moves the map around. "Why are we going to Martin Island?" Miles asks slowly.

"What?" I turn to look at him, but he's already staring at me with a guarded look. "I didn't know what the island's name was. What's on the island, Miles?"

He licks his lips and places my phone on a holder in front of him. I glance back at Saint and notice that he's leaned forward, listening to us. "A sex club ran by Los Lobos was recently raided by the Vicario Cartel. They killed all of the men working in the club and took the women sex workers to sell in the skin trade." Miles avoids looking at us as he starts the helicopter and pulls on his headset.

Saint and I follow, and as soon as Saint can speak to him, he barks, "How the fuck do you know all of that?"

"Because I was there with Briar. I snuck her out the back and flew her here." He lifts the cyclic and we start to rise into the air, the branches on the trees sweeping wildly as the propellers cascade wind towards them.

Oh, shit.

"Did you track the plates?" Miles asks after I fill him in on what we know so far about Allie.

The waters are still in the Sound as we fly high above it. "Yeah, they were stolen."

"So we have no idea who's on Martin Island," he pauses. "And you thought it would be a great idea to just roll up with the five of us." Miles glares ahead of us as he flies his helicopter.

"We needed everyone else at the clubhouse. Shit might be starting up for us soon." I squint my eyes, thinking I saw a small ripple in the water with and a black fin peeking through the surface. My heart breaks into two at the sight. I need to find her.

"Seems like it already has," Miles says.

15

ALLIE

I CAN FEEL MY HEARTBEAT IN MY BRAIN, AND MY MOUTH FEELS LIKE the Sahara. Oh, God. My head hurts so bad.

I raise my hands to my head, and my eyes snap open when my arms don't move. I stare up at the hard plastic of the zip tie as the stinging split of them finally sets in.

I look around the dark room in confusion. This room isn't mine. The metal headboard that I'm tied to isn't mine. The tangy odor of rust hangs thick in the air.

Oh, God... the man at the clubhouse. He drugged me.

My head jolts to the other side of the room at the sound of zip ties scraping against wood.

"Did they take you too?" a fragile voice asks.

"What?" I squint, trying to see through the dark room. She shifts again, and I see the outline of her. "Yeah, they took me too. Who are they? How long have you been here?"

She sighs, "Not long, I don't think. My name's Reyna."

"I'm Allie—" I'm interrupted by the door creaking open. A sliver of light filters into the room, but it is soon blocked by a large body entering the room.

I frantically search my dark surroundings for anything that I can use to help me, but I can't see anything. The girl disappears into the darkness, curling into a ball and hiding herself. I don't blame her. I jerk my legs up, trying to become as small as possible like she did.

I'm truly fucked.

"Oh, darn you're awake," the guy says, his face hidden in the dark. "That's okay, fighting gets me just as hard."

My eyes snap shut as he lunges for me, gripping my thighs with a painful grip and yanking them straight.

I try to kick and trash, but he holds onto me, his nails digging into my skin and the zip ties slicing into my wrists deeper. Reluctantly I open my eyes, the bottoms filling with tears as I see the pure glee in his.

He sits on my thighs, letting all of his weight restrain me under him, and a sob catches in my throat as he reaches for the button of my shorts.

He licks his lips as he drags my shorts down my legs. The denim scraps against my skin, and a whimper leaks out from my throat as I try unsuccessfully to get away from this man. There's nowhere I can go.

He scoots back and sits on my shins as his slimy hands slithers up my thigh. "I was told we could try you out before we sell you off." I want to puke and cry and scream, but the only thing I do is stare at the ceiling, because if this is going to happen, then I won't let him have my fear.

He can't have my fear, because when I get out of here—and I *will* get out of here—my men will tear him limb from limb, and I don't want him to remember my crying face before he dies. I won't give him the satisfaction of knowing that he broke me.

That's the thought that I hold onto: making it back to Saint and Mason. Because I fought too damn hard to not be happy with them for the rest of my life.

His hand travels over my waist and up my stomach, slipping

under Saint's tee shirt. Right before he reaches my breast, the door slams open.

"Josh, come on! Boss is landing!" a man shouts as he stands in the doorway.

Josh's hand stills on my sweating skin and he licks his lips as he stares down at me. "I'll be right back, beautiful," he says before pushing off of the bed and leaving the room.

I gulp in deep breaths of rusty air and pull my legs up to my chest as tears stream down my face, falling over my temples and wetting my hair. "Haunted" by Laura Les starts to play loudly through wherever we are, so loud that I can barely hear myself think. Which is good, because my thoughts are scary, but I also can't hear if anyone is coming back, and that's terrifying.

I beg to whoever is listening—the universe, God, any fucking deity—to save me. Give me something to save myself. I've never been more terrified in my entire life.

A quick succession of gunshots pierce the air, and I snap my head towards the closed door. I know my Outlaws are here for me. I knew they wouldn't stop until they found me, and they did. I can feel that my men are close to me. I can feel the pull in my heart that leads me to them. I don't bother screaming though, there's no chance they would hear me over the music.

I listen as shots ring back and forth, popping off at different times, and sometimes overtop of each other. I can't do anything but lie here and listen.

One last gunshot, and the music cuts off abruptly.

"Allison!" Saint bellows from somewhere behind the door.

I trash against my restraints, the ties cutting deeper into my wrists and ankles. "Saint! Mason!" I yell at the top of my lungs, my throat burning with the force. "Saint! Mason!" I scream again.

The door bursts open, the door handle sticking in the wall behind it with the force.

A light shines on blonde hair, backlighting my Saint, my savior. More tears pour down my cheeks as Saint rushes to the bed, Mason one step behind him.

Saint's eyes flare as he takes me in, but he quickly turns. "Get the fuck out!" he shouts at the door while Mason steps around him and takes me in as well.

"Miles has a knife, hang on." He turns and runs out of the room.

Saint kneels beside me on the floor, his big hands slowly reaching up to cup my cheeks. "Did they do anything to you?" he chokes out, staring down at the mattress in front of him.

"No," I cry, wishing with everything that I could hug him.

"Allie," Saint warns, picking his head up, his eyes shining with unshed tears.

"No," I say more sternly. "You got here in time."

He lowers his head again, shaking it. "I'll never forgive myself for letting this happen to you."

I'll never tell him what almost happened. It doesn't matter anymore, because they got here in time.

Mason sprints back into the room and gently cuts the zip ties from my wrists first. I bolt up from the bed the minute my hands are free and wrap them around Saint's neck. He holds onto me like a lifeline, and my grip is just as fierce.

Mason stares at me, his chest rising quickly and his sea-green eyes wide, and I let go of Saint to reach for him.

He catches me as I fling myself at him, his arms wrapping like steel bands around my waist.

"Save her!" I urge Saint.

"Who?" Saint asks, looking around the room and finding Reyna, staring wide-eyed at us on a small bed, much like mine. "Oh shit," he breathes. "Leo! Get in here!"

"Fuck, Solnyshko. What did they do to you?" Mason whispers into my hair, and I hear his voice crack.

"Nothing, I'm okay. I just need both of you." I pick my head up to look at Saint, who keeps looking back and forth between me and Reyna.

Saint finally pushes off of the ground and grabs my shorts. He unbuttons them and steps toward us, kneeling in front of us to offer them to me. Leaning against Mason, I step into the shorts and watch Saint.

He stares up at me with every emotion under the sun—so much love and pain—it hurts.

"What's up, Prez?" Leo asks, walking into the room.

He tosses Miles's knife to him. "Get her out, she's going with us." He gestures toward Reyna.

Pushing off of Mason, I walk with Leo to Reyna. I can see her better in the light. Her bright blue eyes are bloodshot, and black makeup trails down her face, like she's been crying. I'm sure she has. She's in her bra and underwear with her wrists tied to the bed like I was, but her ankles are free. Her long, jet-black hair hangs limp around her face. Regardless of that, she's still stunning. Plump lips, a small nose, and alluring eyes. I'm stunned by her beauty.

Reyna cowers at the head of the bed as Leo and I reach her.

Kneeling down beside her, I place my hands on the dirty mattress next to her. "It's okay, Reyna. These are my boyfriends and their friends. They're going to get us out of here. Nothing will happen to you with us."

Tears pour down her smooth face, but she nods, looking up to Leo.

For the first time—I think ever—Leo is silent. No jokes, no flirting. He just stares into Reyna's eyes as he cuts her wrists free from the bedpost and takes off his hoodie, handing it to her to put on. I guess that's a good thing though, considering the circumstances. I'm just surprised he could be mature for once.

"Can you walk?" he asks in the gentlest tone I've ever heard him use. If I wasn't standing next to him, I would have thought someone else said it. She nods quickly.

"I think Miles has a first aid kit in the helicopter. We can bandage you both up in there." Mason's voice is rough behind me.

"Helicopter?" I ask, turning around. "Where are we?"

Saint steps around him and picks me up, cradling me in his strong arms. "Some island in the Sound. You both need to be prepared for when we leave this room."

"Why?" I ask, panic starting to set in again. Did they take more people from the club? Did something happen to Reese or Huntley?"

"We didn't leave any survivors, but this place was already pretty fucked up before we got here," Saint says as he steps through the door. The rust smell is even stronger out here, and as he steps over bodies in various states of decay, I realize that the rust smell wasn't ever rust, but blood. So much blood that it coats the walls like paint and the floors like a polish.

This was a massacre.

My arms circle Saint's neck as I hold onto him tightly. I bury my face into his neck until the smell of blood is almost gone. When I pick my head up, I can see the water beyond the small island, only big enough for the large building and a wide grassy area. How long was I out for? I don't remember anything after seeing that guy in the compound parking lot.

Saint carries me all the way to the helicopter. He doesn't let me go until Mason is settled in next to us in the helicopter, and Saint passes me to him as someone hands him a medical kit.

"Thanks, Miles," Saint says quietly as he opens it and roots around inside.

Leo is sitting on the other side of Mason with Reyna sitting silently in his lap, and Jack is in the front with the guy that I guess has to be Miles. I've heard of him since he helped with Reese's stalker and is friends with Mase, but I'd never met him.

Saint starts to bandage my wrists as we fly over the Sound.

"Allie," Saint says softly, keeping his eyes on his steady hands. "Did you recognize the guy that took you?"

"No." I shake my head. "He was wearing a mask." Turning around, I face Reyna. "Did you know them?" I ask.

She shakes her head, pieces of her black hair falling over her slim shoulders. "No. They picked me up outside of my house. It was dark, and I never saw them."

"You can stay with us. We'll protect you." I look at both of my guys, mentally telling them to agree.

Reyna wraps her arms around herself. "You guys don't even know who took us. I'd really rather just go home."

"Okay." I nod. "We can take you home."

"Everyone," Saint speaks. "Back to the clubhouse when we land. We need to have Church again. Leo, take Reyna home."

"Got it, Prez," Leo replies.

"Yup," Jack answers quietly.

16

SAINT

"Take her upstairs and stay with her. I'll be up there once Church ends," I tell Mason as I help Allie off of my bike. Her arms were wrapped so tight around me the entire ride home that I could barely breathe. That still didn't ease my panic over almost losing her. Killing those hired dummies didn't do anything to diminish my anger at all. That probably won't ever go away, even when I kill whoever took her. This should have never happened, not to my Queen.

I hate myself for ever letting her feel an ounce of pain or terror. I should have left more guys here. It had to have been Los Lobos. I mean, they owned the island that they took Allie too. Killing our President wasn't enough, they had to kidnap my woman.

I should have taken Allie far away the day that I picked her up at the hotel bar. I should have left behind this life, the club, and just taken her away.

But by that time, I don't know if she would have left with me. She was already falling for Mason. He would have been in the back of her mind for the rest of her life with me. A 'what if' that she would always wonder about in the quiet of the night, as she was looking out of the window while washing dishes, or folding laundry. The times that her mind would wander to what her life would have been like with him in it.

She won't agree, but I'd rather have only a portion of her heart than ever see her hurt like tonight.

Walking in and seeing her tied to a bed, half naked, was probably worse than walking in and finding her dead, because I know that she suffered something, even if she says we got there in time. She saw and felt things that she will always have to live with. That's got to be worse than death.

Mase nods, wrapping his arm around Allie's shoulders and leading her toward the clubhouse. I watch her tuck her head into his chest and walk with him. She doesn't seem to be too badly down. She's frightened, obviously, but she's aware. I can still see her fire in her eyes, and the love when she looks at Mason and I. She's still in there.

Jack walks to the clubhouse, and I follow behind him slowly, scanning the compound for any sign of danger. I'm even more on edge now that I know someone got in here.

Nox fixed the gate while we were gone, and he's on rounds duty while we have church. After that, we'll take turns. I'm not letting anyone else get in here. Especially since we kicked shit off with Los Lobos today.

When I step into the clubhouse, I catch a crying Reese letting go of Allie, and Mason pulling her back under his arm and taking her up the stairs. Reese turns around and falls into Cale's chest, holding onto the back of his shirt tightly as she cries into it. Cale closes his eyes and holds his wife. Fuck, his *wife*.

I never should have made such a rash call today when two of our brothers have wives, and Mason and I have Allie.

But Ronan...

I'm conflicted on how I feel.

I wish I could talk to him. Ask him what he would have done. How he's doing, wherever he is. I wish I could tell him that I miss him, and I wish I could tell him about Allie, and how happy she's made me, even when I tried so hard to not be.

Cale catches me watching, and whispers something to Reese. She nods and pulls away, heading for the bar, where Huntley is sitting and talking to one of the cut sluts. Callum bows his head to me and steps into the Chapel. I want to get this over with and get upstairs to our girl.

Everyone is in their seats waiting for me, except for Mason and Leo of course.

"I'm glad you got your girl back, Prez. Is she okay?" Tobi asks as I take my seat at the head of the table.

Sighing, I slouch in my chair. "Eventually."

"Does she know who took her?" Finn's black baseball cap is turned backwards and he stares down at a joint that he's lighting. He notices me staring at him and hands me the lit joint.

I take it from him and take a long hit, letting the calming feeling wash over me. "No. He was wearing a mask, and another girl that was taken didn't see the guys either, but it had to be Los Lobos. They were on their island. There weren't any Lobos there though, they all looked like junkies."

"But why take her to some island that could be traced back to them easily?" Cale asks from the other side of me.

Shaking my head, I take another hit and hand the joint back to Finn. "I don't know. Miles said the club that was on the island was run by Los Lobos. He said the Vicario Cartel recently came in and took everybody out and sold the girls working there. Maybe they thought no one would consider the island since the club has been shut down." I inwardly cringe when I remember the scene we walked in on. Fuck. "It was fucked up. I haven't ever seen that level of brutality, and I don't ever want to see something like that again." Men were decapitated, their stomachs sliced open and their guts spilling out, trails of blood following behind them from where they tried to drag themselves to safety before dying of blood loss or a machete to the back of the head. Today was a rough fucking day. "I can't fucking understand why they wouldn't burry their dead though. To just leave them rotting like that is fucked up."

"Could it be the Cartel?" Nate narrows his eyes.

"We've never had any run-ins with the Vicario Cartel." I shake my head. "I didn't even know they were in the area."

Finn spins his lighter on the table with his middle finger. "I didn't hear of Los Lobos losing any guys. This is quick for them to be coming at us for taking out their leader."

"Miguel wasn't even cold before they came for Allie. That's a pretty fucking quick retaliation," Cale argues.

"The Kings have plenty of reasons to come after us," Nate sneers. "A peace pact wouldn't stop their bitch asses."

"Especially one that we forced them into," Tobi says as he pulls a cigarette out of the pack.

"The Kings have been quiet, besides showing up at a party uninvited." Finn waves away Nate and Tobi's accusation.

"I don't trust them," Nate grumbles.

I listen to all of my brothers, and they all make logical points, but I don't know what's right, and that's really fucking frustrating.

Turning my chair sideways, everyone's eyes snap to me and they stop chattering. "I'll have Mason and Miles watch Los Lobos every move, try to figure out if they step out again. For now, everyone go home and get some sleep. Lock your doors, turn on your alarms, and keep your guns loaded and next to your bed. We don't know if there will be another attack. I want everyone to check in with me in the morning."

Agreements ring out around the table, and I bang the gavel on the wood, ending our meeting.

Everyone files out of the room, and I'm left alone, staring at the wall. I push up from my chair. I have one place that I need to be right now, and it's not in this cursed fucking chair.

17

ALLIE

"I NEED TO SHOWER." I SIGH AS MY FEET WALK ALONG THE familiar, low pile carpet of Mason's bedroom.

I hear the door close behind me as I stand in the middle of the dark room, the light getting cut off from the hallway. "Uhh-hh," Mason says.

Closing my eyes, I let out a silent, shaky breath. "Please, Mason. I need to wash..." I shake my head, trying to push the memory out of my head.

The bedside light clicks on and a moment later, Mason's shoulder brushes against mine as he steps around me. He lifts my wrists with such a gentle touch, it makes my heart ache. "Okay, Solnyshko." He focuses on my dressings. "I think your bandages are waterproof, and Saint can redo them when you're done." He steps backward, his eyes rising to mine and staying there as he leads me into the bathroom behind him.

"Can I help you, or do you need to do this alone?" Mason asks when we step into the attached bathroom.

"You can help," I say, pulling Saint's shirt over my head.

Mason steps back and reaches into the stall, turning the

water on. His bathroom is small, and we lightly bump each other as we quietly undress.

The shower stall starts to fog over, and Mase opens the door and steps in, leaving it open for me.

With a deep breath, I step into the warm steam and see Mason's taut abs and muscular thighs as he tilts his head back, the water running over his dark hair and soaking it.

His head lowers, his eyes trailing over my body slowly. But it isn't with lust. He's checking me for injuries. I know it. I can feel each slow passing of his eyes over my body. He steps to the side, and the water pelts the floor where he was standing. I move forward and feel the relaxing heat of the water slide over my body.

Mason's hand gently grasps my waist before he turns me around, putting my hair under the water.

As he grabs for his shampoo that's behind him, I'm reminded of the night that I washed him, after he killed Vadim.

His strong fingers massage my scalp, and I'm distracted enough that I'm not even upset about having to use his horrid man shampoo.

I'm surrounded by Mason, his presence, his warmth, his scent. My sunshine bleeds his affection into me, and I almost feel whole again. I'm just missing my dark and broody. My rainstorm.

"I'm so sorry, Allie." Mason's whisper can barely be heard over the steady stream of falling water.

"I'm okay, Mase." I stare forward at his tan chest, my eyes tracing his Outlaw tattoo.

"I know you are. You're so strong, Solnyshko. But I won't ever forgive us for letting you be taken." He lightly kisses my forehead. "We wouldn't have survived without you. You're the center of our entire universe."

Finally, I bring my eyes to his beautiful sea-green ones. "And you're both mine. My sun and my moon."

Mason nods resolutely and angles my head back again to rinse the shampoo. He goes about the rest of the motions, putting in the conditioner, rinsing, and washing my body, all without any sensuality.

Maybe that's what I need to completely wash away that man's touch. The touch of my men.

"I'm going to step out and grab us some clothes, okay? Come out when you're ready." Mason kisses my cheek before turning around and opening the shower door.

Turning off the shower, I get out when I hear the click of the bathroom door shutting behind Mason. I wrap the fluffy towel around myself and dry off, taking the second one from the rack to dry my hair.

"this is how you fall in love" by Jeremy Zucker and brent ii plays softly in the bedroom, and I lower my eyebrows at Mason when I hear the soft tune.

"I heard some of the guys in the hallway. I was trying to drown out the noise for you," he answers, leaning back in his gaming chair with a folded pile of clothes in his lap.

He offers them to me: it looks like one of his shirts and a pair of shorts. "I don't want those." I gently shake my head.

Mason stands, but I block his way to his dresser. He's already dressed in a pair of lounge shorts. He lowers his head to look at me, and I slowly let go of the top of my towel, letting it fall to the floor in a heap.

Mason's tongue darts out to lick his lower lip as his gaze wanders down my slightly dripping body. "Allie..." he breathes. "Are you sure?"

Nodding, I take a step toward him. "More than," I answer with conviction. Standing naked in front of him, with his eyes finally taking me in in a way that isn't with sadness or anger, has only made me more sure that this is exactly what i need. I need my men with me. Naked and hot and all mine. I need them to make me feel alive and loved.

In a sudden change of mood, Mason picks me up. Gone are the soft, hesitant touches, and my loving Mason is back.

He turns to carry me to the bed, and I wrap my arms around his shoulders and lean forward to kiss up his neck. He takes one step and then the door to his room opens, both of us jolting apart and Mason turning so his back is to the door.

Luckily for me—or maybe unluckily—the person who intruded on our moment was Saint.

He quickly steps into the room, slamming the door behind him. "If you're going to get Allie naked, lock the fucking door. Anyone could have walked in and seen her!" Saint snaps.

Mason chuckles, his head turned as we both watch Saint from over his shoulder. "Well, since it's just you, you want to join in?"

Saint's eyes narrow. "You two shouldn't be doing anything that I could join in on. Not tonight."

Mase rolls his eyes, looking away from Saint to gaze at me. "She said she wanted this, so I'm going to give her whatever she wants." He turns, taking me to the bed. "Join in or get out, because I'm not stopping until she tells me to." He gently lays me on the bed as he stands, pushing his shorts down and stepping out of them. He's still wearing his boxers, but with the gleam in his eye and the quick look he flicks over to Saint, I think he's trying to ease Saint into the idea.

"Fuck!" Saint sighs, and I can already picture his angry face as he drags his hand down his face. Mason's smirk is all I need to know that Saint is staying in the room with us, though I can't see around Mason's body. "I guess the least I could do is give you some pointers," he says, a moment before I hear Mason's gaming chair swivel around.

"I don't need any," Mason says proudly, his grin splitting his face from ear to ear. He bends down at the waist, his hands gripping my thighs. "Show Sainty how beautiful you are when you cum for me, Solnyshko," is the last thing Mason says before he drops to his knees and a glaring Saint replaces where he was.

My eyes widen when I'm confronted with Saint sitting in the gaming chair at the foot of the bed. His eyes are narrowed as he leans forward, his stare already on mine, making my heart rate pick up to concerning levels.

I can't contain the loud moan that I let out when Mason spreads my pussy lips and licks a long trail from my opening to my clit, with two men's eyes watching me closely.

"Lick her slowly. Savor her," Saint instructs, his eyes never wavering.

Mason follows his orders, lightly and slowly licking the same, long stroke as before. Tossing my head back, I close my eyes tightly. I won't be able to hold on. Not with both of them watching me. Not with Saint directing Mason on how to eat me out.

"Uh-uh," Mason tsks. "Eyes on us, babe."

Picking my head up again, I look at both of them before my eyes stay on Saint.

"How does she taste, brother?" Saint asks, his elbows resting on his knees as he leans forward.

"Fucking perfect," Mason groans, taking another lick.

"Suck on her clit and finger her until she cums," Saint orders. I already feel my stomach quivering, so it won't take him long to do as Saint commands. "Is she about to cum?" Saint asks, his eyes finally leaving mine and roaming down my naked chest.

"Mmhmm," Mason hums against my clit, and I let out a shriek of pleasure.

Saint leans back in the chair with an evil smirk on his face. "Then stop. She's had enough for tonight."

I snap my eyes down to Mason as he watches me. "Not happening." Mason pulls away from me, but before I can protest that this is not ending here, he switches places with me, tossing me on top of him with his hands on my waist. "Ride me, Solnyshko."

Looking over my shoulder, I smirk at a glaring Saint, and turn back around. "You have to get rid of these first." I snap the band of his boxers against his slim waist.

Mason lifts his hips underneath me and pushes his boxers down his long legs, kicking them the rest of the way off and spreading his legs as he lays back down.

Palming his large cock, I line it up with my pussy and slowly sink down onto him. He fills me perfectly, and I immediately start bouncing on his dick, putting a wave into my hips with the knowledge that Saint is watching my every move.

Mason is talented with his tongue, and could easily have gotten me off, but the fact that Saint was watching made it infinitely sexier. It would have only been better if he had joined in instead of barking out orders.

These men know my body better than I do and can get me off in record time, and I fucking love it.

"Fuck, you feel so good, babe," Mason moans loudly. The sounds of our bodies slapping together and our combined moans fill the room.

Mason's hands slide from my waist up my sides, and he brings me forward until my elbows are pressing on either side of his head and I'm pressed to his hot chest, staring into his beautiful eyes. His hands glide back down my body and he cups my ass, squeezing my cheeks. Mason spreads my ass apart, giving Saint a front row seat to his dick, sliding in and out of me slowly, as he takes over fucking me. "Look at this tight little asshole, Saint," Mason says loudly. "Why don't you come fill it up with me and show Allie who she belongs to." My cheeks heat as I stare wide-eyed down at Mason, but despite my blush, my pussy wants exactly that, and it lets Mason know by pulsing around him. Just imagining taking both Saint and Mason is enough to make me cum. He groans, "Oh, you want that baby? You want Sainty to fuck your ass while you ride my dick? You want to be marked as Outlaw property and walking funny tomorrow?" I moan, the start of an orgasm rolling over me. "Saint you better hurry up if you want in on this, our girl is about to burst."

The room turns eerily quiet as Mase and I wait for Saint to either storm out or join us. Finally, I hear the faint sound of a zipper and clothes falling to the floor behind me.

Goosebumps erupt over my ass and up my back as I feel a warm breath ghost over my behind. A wet tongue flattens over my asshole and I jolt forward with a scream. Mason hisses underneath me as my pussy clenches around him.

"Lube is in the drawer," he grunts, sounding like he's in pain.

Turning my head, I watch Saint walk around the bed, open the bedside drawer, and grab a small bottle of lube. His thick cock stands erect as he slowly pumps it.

Once behind me again, he rubs lube over my asshole generously. The cold, slippery liquid makes me jolt again, and Mason groans. "Hurry up, I'm about to cum."

"Amateur," Saint says under his breath, slipping a finger inside me and slowly finger fucking me with it. "Mason is the only man I will share you with, Allie. Ever." He adds another finger. "You wanted this, you wanted the both of us, now I'm going to make you pay for it. You're never going to be able to mutter another man's name." Saint slams his thick cock into my ass, the painful stretch making me scream but also triggering the orgasm that I've been holding at bay.

"You're so beautiful, taking both of us," Mason moans, his arms wrapping tightly around me. "I can feel Saint fucking you,

Solnyshko," Mason says into my ear as Saint fucks me hard from behind.

"She's our dirty little whore, isn't she?" Saint asks, his hand coming down hard on my ass as he fucks me relentlessly. "Maybe one day, Mason and I will both fuck your greedy little pussy together." Another slap rings down hard. "Not today though, you have to earn that, my Queen."

Saint's harsh words mixed with Mason's will be my undoing. The stretch of the both of them, the way they alternate their thrusts so I'm never empty—I'm in fucking heaven.

A heaven filled with the most dirtily, disgusting sounds, and the scents of both of my men. I'm not normally one to want to just lay around and be fucked, but with both of them fucking me, I have no choice but to lay here and take everything they're giving out. And oh, fuck, are they giving it all.

I feel like a boneless heap of sensation. My pebbled nipples and pulsing clit scrape against Mason as I'm jostled forward by Saint. Saint's hands roam over my back, occasionally slapping my ass, which causes me to tighten both holes, in turn, making my guys moan and hiss in response; which is probably why Saint keeps doing it.

"Do you want it harder, baby? I can feel your pussy tightening again." Mason picks up his pace under me.

"Is your greedy pussy going to cum again around Mason's cock? You're such a slut." Saint slams his hips into me, pushing me into that next orgasm.

"Fuck, fuck, fuck!" Mason shouts as he wildly thrusts into me, all thought of Saint abandoned.

I feel his hot cum filling me a second later as he relaxes into the bed, his face softening as he takes deep breaths.

"My turn," Saint whispers into my ear before rolling us over so he's on his back with my back on top of him. "Suck her clit," Saint orders Mason.

Mason lazily flops over and positions himself in between Saint and I's legs as Saint opens my legs wide and fucks my ass.

Mase sucks my clit hard and runs his fingers through his cum, which is slipping out of me. He picks it up on his fingers and pushes it back into me.

"Mmm, I love your pussy, but this tight ass is sweet too," Saint moans. "This is our ass, Allie." He lets go of one of my legs and pushes Mason's face away from my pussy. "And this is our pussy." He slaps my clit hard, causing a scream and another orgasm to sweep through me with a surprising intensity. "That's it, my Queen. Take my cum like the dirty little whore that you are."

Saint's body stills beneath me, and I rest all of my weight on his chest. I've officially been fucked senseless, and I don't think I have any strength to move.

"Take her to the shower," Saint breathes heavily. "I'll be in, in a second."

Mason chuckles, his easy going smile lighting up the dim room. "Old man," Mason jokes, sliding his arms under my legs and back and lifting me off of Saint. "Bring the lube!" he calls over his shoulder. "I call her ass this time!"

Oh, God. I'm going to die in the shower. Death by dicks.

18

SAINT

Watching Allie hobble to the bathroom fills me with a dirty sense of pride. We literally fucked her until she was walking funny. That's something to be proud of.

Laying in bed alone with my brother, however, not as much. So with that thought, I roll out of my side—nope, not claiming a side in Mason's bed—and throw on my jeans from yesterday. I pick up my shirt and examine it, and it's covered in blood. Of course.

"You can take one of mine. Second drawer from the top," Mason yawns, rolling over and pulling the comforter over his head.

Walking over, I pull open the drawer and grab the first shirt I see. Since I'm up, I might as well go down and make us something for breakfast, since we didn't get a lot of sleep last night.

Sharing Allie with Mason last night was surprisingly easy. There wasn't any jealousy or feeling like one of us was a third wheel.

It felt natural. Like it is what we should have been doing all along. And that weirds me the hell out.

I never would have foreseen myself sharing my girlfriend

with another man—especially beyond the bedroom—but I know that this wouldn't work without one of us. It's the three of us or none of us, and I guess that's what reassures me that I'm doing the right thing. That Allie and Mason won't just wake up one day and decide that instead of three being a party, it's now a crowd, and drop me.

However, the same goes for Allie and me. Although I'd love nothing more than to have her all to myself all the time, I know that her heart won't be whole unless we're both in it.

I hate that it took me so long to realize that she wasn't rejecting me, but trying to find a way to make this work for all of us. But I wasn't in my right mind then.

My grief made me more hostile, less open to hearing what others needed. It's like I was in a flight or fight mindset, but my only option was to fight. With everyone, including myself.

That's what everyday felt like: a fight with myself, and I never knew which part of me would win. The side that wanted to end it all or the side that wanted to fight for a life with Allie. The life that Ronan wanted me to have.

Thumping down the stairs with bare feet, I tie my hair up in a bun at the back of my head and flip the switch to turn the lights on in the main room.

A long, strained groan comes from the couch against the back wall, and I look over to see Nate rolling off of the couch. "You slept here last night?" I ask, walking the opposite direction to the kitchen behind the bar.

"Yeah," he answers, his voice thick with sleep. "Fucking Jack said I had too much to drink and hid my keys." He swipes at his eyes as he stumbles over to the bar.

A silver ring of keys glistens under the light of the bar, sitting in a bowl with chip crumbs. Picking them up, I jingle them in the air. "These your keys?"

Nate shakes his head. "Little shit." He catches them as I toss them to him. "I'm just going to grab my extra pack of cigs. Nothing cures a hangover like some nicotine."

Turning my back to him, I raise my hand in the air, waving him out, and walk into the kitchen.

The tile is cold under my bare feet as I walk to the refrigerator, deciding what I should make Mase, Allie, and I for breakfast... and I guess Nate, too, since he's here and awake. My fingers wrap around the stainless steel handle and I pull open the door.

My heart rate kicks up as a loud crash and the sound of glass shattering comes from outside of the kitchen. Slamming the stainless steel door closed, I turn around and quickly walk into the main room, but as I look around, I find it empty. Nate left the door to the lot open, so I walk that way when gunshots ring out from outside.

I hop over the bartop and grab the AR that is stashed in the cabinet under the bar. I hope the shots wake everyone else up, because I don't have time to. Nate is out there, and I don't have a good feeling about what I'll find when I step out of the door.

Maybe it's intuition, but I think it's just being realistic. Los Lobos are after us, and we made a big play yesterday. They're back for another pound of flesh.

My feet slap the hardwood as I run through the main room of the clubhouse, and I come to an abrupt stop when I see the mayhem that is the parking lot. I barely register the guys climbing out of a black pickup that was driven through our gate, or the sounds of my brothers running through the clubhouse, shouting.

All I can focus on is the bike that's on fire and other small fires that are burning on the ground, the shattered glass and drenched rags a clear sign of molotov cocktails.

Nate is lying next to the burning bike, blood starting to pool around his head, and a skinny Lobo stands over him with his gun aimed at Nate's head.

I raise the AR and aim for the skinny fucker. Two shots, and he falls to the ground beside Nate. His buddies immediately take aim at me, and I duck behind a trash barrel, just as I hear Jack shout to take cover.

Jack and Nox peek around the door frame and exchange shots with the two guys that are huddled on the opposite side of their truck. I stare at Nate, trying to see if his chest moves, but I can't tell from here with everything going on around me.

I have to get to him. I stand up, ignoring the very obvious signs that this is a terrible idea, and fire at the truck. The guys notice that I'm not covered, and they peek out. Jack finishes off the two remaining guys as I act as a target while running to Nate.

In the back of my mind, I knew that was a stupid plan, but I had to get to Nate, and every second I waited for a clear shot, he could be bleeding out.

But when I reach Nate, I realize that I was too late.

The man aiming a gun at him had already shot him when I found them. Right between the eyes. There's no saving him.

Even still, my knees hit the pavement hard and my fingers dig into his skin as I search for a pulse on the side of his neck.

I pull my trembling fingers away when a hand grips my shoulder. "He's gone, Saint," Nox says gently.

I know he's right, but I can't bear the thought. What did I do?

For the second time, I think that I made the wrong call in getting vengeance.

By avenging my dearest friend, my girlfriend was kidnapped and another brother was killed.

Another Outlaw funeral. Less than two months apart.

"He's alive!" Jack shouts from beside me on the ground.

Hope blossoms deep in my stomach for half a second, before

the sputtering at his feet knocks me in the chest. He meant the guy that I shot was alive. Not Nate.

"Get him inside and on a table. We need answers before he dies!" I snap. "Nox, check the others for survivors."

Nox runs toward the truck, and Jack and I move around to lift the Lobo.

He groans when I roughly grab under his arms and Leo grabs his waist and thighs. We quickly carry him to the clubhouse.

The morning is silent around us again, the only sound is the hurried footsteps of Jack and I and the wheezing breathing of the man we're carrying.

"What's going on?" Mason asks as we get through the threshold of the clubhouse.

I quickly scan the room and find Allie waiting at the stairs, her eyes wide and hair a mess. They must have ran down after hearing the commotion too.

Her arms are wrapped around herself. She's wearing one of Mason's shirts and her shorts from yesterday. At least she put on pants before coming down. I don't need another reason to fucking lose it today.

"Take Al upstairs," I say to Mason, then I look up at Jack. "I got him, bring Nate inside. He doesn't deserve to lay outside like an animal."

"What can I do?" Mason asks as he walks behind me, pausing to look at the man on the table.

"Call Richards and get him out here; we have to report Nate's death. Then call everyone else. We're going on lockdown until this is over."

19

MASON

I FINALLY GET ALLIE BACK UPSTAIRS, AFTER SHE WENT AND checked on Saint, of course. He's shutting down again. I can see it in his eyes. Losing Nate is fucking with his head. He's never going to let the last two days go—What happened to Allie and now Nate—he's blaming himself.

I called everyone, and they're all moving into the clubhouse within the next hour. Richards is on his way here to falsify Nate's death record. We don't need anyone looking into a shooting on our property. Nox and Jack are getting ready to bury the two guys that are lying dead in our parking lot. And Saint is playing doctor downstairs with our new hostage.

What the fuck?

I wasn't as close to Nate as the other guys, but I still feel his absence. He was my brother, and he was always there when someone needed to talk. He didn't treat the younger guys any differently than the older ones. He was just everyone's friend. I'm going to miss him.

Saint wanted me to stay in my room with Allie, but I can't sit around and do nothing. I need to help the club somehow.

So I'll help the only way I know how.

Allie pulls up a chair next to me at my computer, and even though she has no idea what's going on, she still looks over my shoulder and watches me work.

I have a few leads I can go through.

Ronan was told that Los Lobos killed Michelle Davis. I can look into that, though I don't know how far I'll get since the FBI has been investigating it as well, and they've come up empty handed.

I can try to trace the burner Ro was texting.

I don't know where to start on who took Peyton, and I don't know if they were the same people who took Allie, but I think it's a pretty fair assumption that they were.

The last one seems like the easiest to track right now.

I pull up security footage from the night that Peyton was picked up from Second, and I wait for the pickup. It pulls up just as Peyton steps out of the club, and I watch with an eerily familiar sense of deja vu as a man wraps Peyton up in his arms and wrestles her into a pickup—a pickup that is the exact same as the one that Los Lobos tossed Allie into.

Mother fucker.

I recognize the dent on the back bumper. The same people who took Allie also took Peyton and beat the shit out of her, putting her in the hospital, and now with Mikhail fucking Belov. I'm still not over that last part. Who would have thought? I wonder how she's doing.

"Another girl was taken?" Allie squeaks, and her soft voice causes me to jump. I was so enthralled with my own thoughts.

I spin toward her, blocking the screen from her view. "It was Peyton, the bartender. She was taken the night that Saint came back from New York." *You know, the night Saint killed your dad.* I definitely leave that out, though. "She was dropped off the next morning at the gate, and Nox took her to the hospital."

Allie's eyes widen. "Is she okay?"

"Yeah." I nod. "Saint sent her to stay with Mikhail," I say slowly, watching several emotions pass over her beautiful face before she shoves the rolling chair out from under her and stands, stomping toward the door.

I think I just sold out Saint... too bad I don't feel twisted up about it. Serves him right for all of the shit he put Allie through.

Allie slams the door open and stomps into the hallway. Shit, on second thought, all three of us are supposed to be a team, so I should probably go down and help him out.

20

SAINT

Upon examination, I've found that the Lobo has a through and through in his shoulder, which is good. However, the bullet in his stomach is staying there, which means I don't have a lot of time to get answers before this guy is joining his friends in a grave out at the cabin.

I apply a bandage and pressure to it in order to slow the blood flow.

Nox and Jack come back inside after putting the bodies away. Jack gets right to work, bringing me smelling salts and some kitchen knives. We don't interrogate at the clubhouse, so none of our tools are here.

"Get me the blowtorch from the kitchen too," I demand, unscrewing the top on the salts. Nox stands off to the side, observing everything with a guarded expression. This is his first interrogation, and this will prove if he's really in this for life or not, but I don't have the time to coddle him through this. It's sink or swim.

"Saint Viotto!" Allie yells, storming down the stairs. She halts to a stop at the bottom when she sees the man on the table and me standing over him, holding a bandage to his gut. She blinks slowly with her mouth agape.

"I don't have time for whatever you're about to yell at me for, Allie. Go back upstairs."

Just then, Jack walks out with the blowtorch, setting it down next to me on the table. "Are you going to save him?" she asks.

Shaking my head, I stare at her out of the tops of my eyes. "Nope, so turn around and go back to Mason."

Allie turns on her heel without another word, and I let out a sigh of relief. That was easier than I expected.

The man coughs as he comes to, and he groans loudly when the pain hits his conscious form.

"I'm going to reason with you, Lobo. I dropped out of medical school before I got to see my surgery rotation. I'd love nothing more than to cut you open with a butcher knife and fish this bullet out of your intestines. Unfortunately for you, we don't have any anesthetic. So, what's your choice? A back alley surgery or a bullet to the brain?" I push a finger into his bullet wound, causing a scream to erupt from him.

"What do you want?" he wheezes.

I love when I get my way. I beam a cheshire smile down at him. "Just one thing. Are Los Lobos framing us for Michelle Davis's murder?" One question is all he has time for.

The man shakes his head, fat tears falling from his eyes. "They'll kill my family."

"*I'll* kill your family if you don't talk. Do you really think you can stand in my way? I have everything I need at my disposal to find your family," I seethe.

He coughs and more blood spills from his mouth. "Yes, we did. And then they found out and said they would give us your territory if we worked with them." His voice sounds wet.

"They, who?" I bark, leaning over him as he gets closer to death.

"I don't know," he wheezes. "White guys, they look like you."

I roll my eyes, annoyed. He's not helping me at all. I already knew they were framing us—not concretely, but I knew. He hasn't told me anything new, only given me more questions. "Who?" I shout in his face.

"Protect my family." His voice is a weak whisper.

I suck my lips between my teeth, letting them go audibly. "Fuck your family. You didn't give a shit when you were gunning mine down in an alley or kidnapping my girl." I glare into his wet eyes as a tear rolls down his face. That was the last thing he said before his eyes unfocused on me and his wheezing breaths stopped.

21

SAINT

"Church. Now," I say as I open Mason's door. He and Allie are both sitting at his computer and they turn their heads at the sound of my voice.

"We need to talk." Allie pushes away from the desk, standing and crossing her arms.

Shaking my head, I lean against the door frame. "After, my Queen."

"Saint," she warns, cocking her head. Mason kisses her soft, blonde hair, stepping around her and toward me.

"After. This is important." I keep my voice and mouth even. I don't want to fight with her, but whatever she's so pressed about does not compare to what we have to discuss. Allie makes an irritated noise, but I shut the door anyway and turn down the hall.

"Did you find anything out?" Mason asks, keeping pace with me.

"A little. I have more work for you." I keep my eyes forward.

He sighs. "Of course you do."

With a flick of Finn's lighter, the fire burns the white paper of the joint, and the sweet smell starts to fill the Chapel.

"My Lobo confirmed what Ronan was doing in the alley. Los Lobos killed Michelle Davis and they are framing us for it." I watch as the cherry blazes, turning brighter.

"So what do we do about that? Can we turn them into the FBI, get them off of our backs?" Leo asks.

My eyes narrow in annoyance. "Do you suggest I call their tip hotline? Explain that Los Lobos shot up our clubhouse in retaliation for murdering their leader, we took one hostage, and threatened his family for his confession?" I cock my head, staring at him. "How well do you think that will go over?"

Leo's eyes slide to the ceiling as he bites his lip. "We could call in an anonymous tip."

"Shut up." I hold my hand up, looking away from him. Sometimes he has a promising future in this life, other times, not so much. "We need proof. Mason, can you get with Miles and look into a connection between Los Lobos and the Senator? It's gotta be connected to him."

"Yeah, Prez," he answers. The dark circles under his eyes are getting darker everyday. I can clearly see the toll Ronan's death has taken on him now. I didn't realize before how much pressure and work I was putting solely on him. I feel a little bad.

"Thank you," I say, ignoring the confused stares from a few of my brothers.

22

ALLIE

IF I THOUGHT THE CLUBHOUSE WAS SMALL BEFORE, IT WAS gigantic compared to when everyone moves in. All but two rooms are taken by members of the club, and the last two are being shared by club girls who don't feel safe enough to go home. What's worse is that Mason, Saint, and I are all sharing Mason's room. One room, one bed, one *bathroom,* and three people. At least Saint and Mason are hygienic guys. Mason is a little messy, but after the first few days of me speed cleaning his desk of the energy drinks and chip bags while he was in the shower, he got the hint. Saint is very anal about his spaces, and I can tell it's driving him crazy to be confined to the clubhouse. He enjoys his space; that's why when he's not tattooing in Purgatory, he's sketching out in the woods. He cleaned up the strip club downstairs and set up his shop there. His clients and club members have been going in and getting tattoos, since there isn't really anything else to do.

I have Reese too, and Huntley. They've made the long days more fun, and my guys have made the nights pass too quickly. I miss them during the day. Mason spends all his time on his computer, chasing down some lead, and Saint works long hours, very rarely coming into Mason's room.

One really great thing has come from this lockdown, though: we all have dinner together, like a family.

I've never had that before. My dad and I would sometimes sit down and eat together, but he was always consumed with a file or his laptop. We never talked about my classes, friends, or really anything. And once he was done eating or he got a call from someone, he would leave without a word.

The ruckus that is our family dinners now fills my heart so full that I think it might burst. I look forward to them every day.

Tonight, Huntley, Wyatt, and I are making parmesan crusted chicken with mashed potatoes and roasted zucchini.

Knock, knock! Someone at the door breaks my mindless scrolling on Tiktok, and I toss my phone down onto Mason's bed. He took a break from his computer to spar with Leo in the boxing ring outside. He said he needed to rest his eyes and his shoulders needed to be worked out. Whatever.

I open the door to find Nox standing in the hallway with a small box. "Hey, Nox!" I smile, holding onto the door.

"This came for Saint and he's with a client." He holds the box up.

I eye the return label, but I didn't recognize the company that sent it. He must've ordered something. "Oh, yeah. I can give it to him." I take the box from Nox and say goodbye.

Setting the box on the desk, I grab my phone and text Saint.

ALLIE:

> Your package was delivered. Nox brought it up to me.

I go back to scrolling, and get suckered into a new skincare website.

SAINT:

I didn't order anything.

SAINT:

Don't touch it, I'll be up in a few minutes.

My eyes switch between Saint's text and the small box sitting on the other side of the room. What if it's a bomb or an eyeball or something? Another attack on the club, or a warning? Who else could they have hurt? Everyone is here. Finn's and Huntley's dads stayed at their homes, instead of coming to the clubhouse. Someone could have gotten to them. Saint's family stayed in Seattle.

The five minutes that Saint takes to come upstairs feels like an hour, and my eyes never leave the petite package.

"Sorry." Saint charges into the room. "I was finishing up with a client. Where is it?" he asks, searching the room with his eyes. He doesn't need me to answer before he finds the box and stalks towards it.

He picks it up and reads the label, his brows pulling together. Saint reaches into his back pocket and pulls out a knife, flicking it open.

I leap off of the bed as his knife plunges into the tape on the top. "What are you doing?" I shout, right before a loud pop explodes from the box.

My eyes widen and I slap my hand over my mouth as hot pink, glitter, confetti dicks rain down on Saint's head.

My body shakes with silent laughter as Saint's eyes stay screwed shut and his chest starts rising quickly.

"What. The. Actual fuck?" He drops the box, swiping at his face where the confetti exploded.

I take a step toward him. The small, pink dicks are stuck in his tied back, blonde hair, and scattered over his shoulders. I had completely forgotten about the prank Mason and I pulled after Saint said something mean one day. "That was actually me." I chuckle, losing the battle of keeping my laughter contained any longer.

"What?" His eyes snap open.

I nod, a wide smile stretching across my face. "Payback. For when you were a giant douche." An idea pops into my head. "Hang on. I need a picture of this!" I excitedly reach into Saint's pocket and pull his phone out, clicking the camera button on the lockscreen.

I angle the camera at Saint's glowering face, a dick pointing right at his left eye, but pause when I see the last picture he took in the little box at the bottom.

It's a picture of me.

"Unlock your phone," I demand, passing his phone to him.

"My password is the day of our first kiss, do you remember it?" He cocks his head, still looking devastatingly handsome, even with the cock confetti. "There's only one right answer here, my Queen." He raises one eyebrow.

Biting my lip, I pull his phone back to me and type in the date of Huntley and Finn's wedding, and his phone opens to his camera roll.

Scrolling through, I see several pictures of me. Ones he took while I wasn't paying attention. Me the night of Sophie's birthday, when Reese was drugged and Saint picked me up from my house and we got pizza. Me at his house, where we had pizza again at his dining room table. The night at Leo's housewarming, in the kitchen with a beer. In the Chapel after we kissed secretly. And in the bathroom downstairs after we fucked during the party.

"You took pictures of me?" I ask, looking at him from under my lashes.

He licks his lips and looks away. "They were all I could have of you at the time."

Setting the phone down on the desk, I take the box from him. "And what will you do with me now that you have more?"

Saint smirks, biting the lifted corner of his lip. "Dirty things, my Queen."

I drop the box and step into his waiting arms. "Show me."

Saint moves quicker than I've ever seen, scooping me up and dropping me onto the desk beside us.

"It's gotta be quick, my Queen. I don't want to share you right now." He reaches for the waistband of my lounge shorts.

Placing my hands on the desk, I lift my ass as Saint strips my shorts and panties down my legs, dropping them on the floor beside him.

He kneels between my legs, lifting one of them and placing my foot on his shoulder.

"Such a pretty, pink pussy," he groans, running his nose down my thigh.

"I thought we were hurrying?" I smirk down at him.

"You're right." He gives me a long lick, a moan slipping from my lips, and he stands, unbuckling his belt and pushing his jeans down enough to slip his cock free.

So much emotion fills his eyes; they do every time he looks at me. And I wish I could decipher all of them, but I know he loves me. "Are you going to fuck me like you hate me again?" I snark, moving my arms behind me and leaning back slightly.

"Shut up." He rolls his eyes and surges into me.

My eyes widen at the shock, my head falling backward with a long moan.

Saint pumps into me with a furious pace. The loud slaps of skin and moans can definitely be heard outside of our room, and things are falling over on the desk due to our pounding against the table.

"Tell me you love me," I moan, wrapping one arm around his neck and holding him against me.

Saint's heavy breaths huff against my neck. "You already know I do."

"Tell me," I demand, my voice steadying.

Saint straightens, his hips slowing. "I love you, Allison Viotto," he says, lifting my ass and rolling his hips into me.

He hits all new spots inside of me and I toss my head back, moaning, "Oh, God!" He does it over and over, but I finally collect enough of my wits to look back at him and speak. "What if I don't take your last name, what if I take Mason's?"

Saint scoffs, leaning back into me and pressing into my pussy deeper. "Allison Underwood? Absolutely not. You'll take my last name." He ruts into me with short, hard thrusts that beat at my cervix and push me toward the edge.

"Faster, Saint," I moan.

"What's the magic word, my Queen?" He chuckles against my shoulder, kissing it gently.

"Now." I grit my teeth. His fingers are steel points in my ass, holding me at his mercy.

"Try again." He licks up my neck and to my ear.

"Please, Saint. Please fuck me faster. I need to cum," I plead.

I can feel Saint's smirk against my skin and I want to punch him for it. "That's my good slut."

I can't help it, that sends me over the edge. I'd consider booking an appointment with my therapist, but damn, I haven't cum this hard since I was being double teamed by Mason and Saint. I refuse to apologize for that.

"Yes, Allie. Milk my cock," Saint groans, and I know it pushed him over the edge too. He likes being dominant and calling me names.

I don't think we would have ever realized that without Saint playing off of Mason's praise.

Saint pulls out of me, tucking himself away and backing away from the desk.

Scooting forward, I slide off of the table and bend over to pick up my panties and shorts, and Saint slaps my ass while I'm bent over.

"Get dressed, my Queen. I'm hungry."

Snapping straight up, I turn around and glare at him. "I should put bleach in your dinner for that!" I swat at his arm, but he shimmies away, dodging me.

Saint cackles as he backs away toward the door. "I'm joking, calm down."

I shake my head at his stupid smirk as he leaves the bedroom. I really should slip some bleach into his food, but he is right, I do need to get downstairs to help Huntley and Wyatt.

In the kitchen, Huntley is mixing the ingredients to coat the chicken and Wyatt is peeling the potatoes.

After washing my hands, I start peeling the zucchini so I can chop them for roasting. The three of us make small conversation while we work—well, mostly Huntley and I. Wyatt doesn't talk to us too much, he mostly just grunts agreements or silently shakes his head while he cooks, but I like him. He's kind and very helpful; he helps before we've even realized we need the help. But we don't push him to talk. Most of the guys here are quiet.

Mason walks in just after the chicken and zucchini have gone into the oven, and the potatoes are on the stove.

His dark hair is hanging in wet pieces over his forehead, and he's in a large, white tee shirt and basketball shorts, with bare feet.

"Smells delicious," he says into my ear, wrapping his arms around my waist from behind and hugging me. "Almost as good as our room smelt when I went in to take a shower."

My cheeks heat, but no one heard him except for me. "Whoops. Sorry." I smile, leaning back into his chest.

"No, you're not," he chuckles, wrapping my tighter into his arms.

"Mase! Are you here to set the table?" Huntley asks, batting her long lashes.

Mason kisses my neck once before letting go. "Sure am!" He collects the plates that Huntley hands him.

"Send in Leo and Jack for the silverware and glasses," she says.

Mason kisses me on the lips before leaving with the plates.

The guys brought Saint's huge outdoor table from his house and set it up outside of the clubhouse. That's where we've been having family dinners for the past few days.

I carry out the large bowl of roasted zucchini and set it in the middle of the table. Finn carried the bowl of potatoes for Huntley, while Wyatt and Jack followed behind us with trays of chicken, and Leo and Nox carried out buckets with ice and beers in them.

This is nothing like I grew up with. Dinner parties had dress codes, and they were in the most pristine places, with views of the city, or the water, or the park. They were catered by exclusive restaurants, or you hired a michelin star chef. There were strictly planned menus, with wines that coordinated with the food. Dinner parties were rarely to catch up with friends, or spend quality time together, they were for business or some ulterior motive disguised as friendship.

The cloudless sky is a light blue that fades into yellow where the sun is setting, and the light reflects off of the tall trees that surround the compound. The air is warm and comfortable, and "Only" by NF and Sasha Alex Sloan plays softly on the outdoor speakers. People slowly trail out of the clubhouse and from chairs scattered outside to the table. Tobi is the slowest of all, and he barely eats the dinners we make. You can tell everyone is grieving the loss of their brother, but he's taking it significantly harder.

Looking around, I realize that this is my life now: these people, this town, my men. I'm happy, even if we are all staying in this tiny clubhouse. These people are my family now, and I'd much rather take them over my selfish mother and father.

Good riddance to my father, I hope he doesn't rest in peace.

23

SAINT

Buzz. Buzz.

"Saint. Your phone." Allie nudges me in the side.

Groaning, I roll over when Allie sits up. "I know," I say through thick layers of sleep.

Allie slides back into Mason's arms as he stirs behind her, and I rub my pec where she was laying before my phone woke us both up. "Who's calling you this late?" she asks quietly.

Lying on my side with my back to her, I open my phone and look at the text that comes in after the call has ended. "Nox. It's club business, I have to go." I toss the sheet off of me, but before I can get up, Allie grabs my hand.

"What's going on?" Her tone tells me she's not in the mood to be jerked around, and honestly, sometimes I wish she would just leave shit alone, but she wouldn't be my Allie if she did. I never thought I would involve my woman in club business, but I'd share every dirty detail if she asked…and she does.

"Nox said he has a lead on the guys that took you and Peyton." I sigh, sitting on the edge of the bed. I can barely see Allie through the darkness, but I know her eyebrows are creasing.

"Take Mason," she urges, letting go of my hand. "Mason, wake up." I feel the bed shake as, I'm assuming, she nudges him like she did me.

"No." I reach out and rest my hand on her hip. "I'll take Finn and Cale. Mason can stay with you." I stroke over the sheet covering her, trying to soothe her enough so I can go.

She sits up and I pull my hand away. I feel the bed dip beside me as she kneels next to me. "Have you guys been doing that on purpose?" she asks, her tone slightly cutting.

"Doing what?" I play dumb. I know exactly what she's getting at.

"Always making sure one of you is with me." Her face inches closer, her narrowed, mint eyes coming into view.

Smirking, I answer. "Of course not, you were alone that one time that Mason was working out and I was working. Or the times you cook dinner with Huntley and Wyatt."

Her blond hair brushes past me as she shakes her head. "No, one of you always shows up shortly after."

"Shhhh." I place my hand on the back of her neck and pull her the rest of the way toward me. "Just go back to sleep. I'll be right back." I press my lips to her forehead and I kiss her.

Her warm arms wrap around my neck. "Please be safe," she whispers, looking into my eyes.

I kiss her, long and slow, and determined. "I will," I promise, pulling away from her.

She lets me go, and I quietly get dressed in the blackness and head for the door.

I turn around and take one last look at Allie before I leave. She's cuddled up with Mason, but I can feel her eyes watching me. I know she'll wait until I come back, and she won't sleep until I'm in bed with them again.

Speaking of beds, we need a bigger one. Even in a king, the three of us are packed together like sardines.

Outside of Cale's room, I lift my hand to pound on the door, but I stop short, remembering that it's not just Cale in his room anymore. His wife is sleeping in there with him. Fuck...I never stopped to think about the fact that two of our brothers are married with Old Ladies. I thought Allie and I might eventually get married, but I don't know now...where could she marry two men? Would she even want to?

Nope. I'm not going there tonight, it's too much of a headache for fucking three A.M.

So instead of banging on the door until Cale wakes up, I call him instead. It takes two phone calls, but on the second one—right before I was about to hang up and pound on the door instead—he finally answers.

Finn wakes up on the first call immediately, but that's probably because he's used to being a light sleeper. He doesn't let many people in on it, but he can be a bit paranoid.

We meet downstairs after they've gotten dressed and said whatever they needed to say to their Old Ladies.

Cale's blonde hair is sticking up in every direction, and he's wearing black sweats and a black hoodie, but he's here. "Where are we going?" he asks, his voice thick with sleep.

Finn looks completely awake, in jeans, a black, long sleeved shirt, and a backwards ball cap.

"Some warehouse by the docks. Nox said he's hiding out, keeping watch," I answer, heading for the Chapel.

"How did he find them?" Finn asks, following behind me.

Shaking my head, I open the door and walk to the gun cabinet. "I have no idea, but we can ask when we get there."

Cale takes the ARs that I hand him, his eyes looking more awake than before. "He's just trying to earn his top rocker."

"That's a hell of a way to get it. Finding the guys who kidnapped the Prez's girl," Finn agrees.

I shove magazines and bullets at Finn. "If he found the guys who kidnapped Allie, I'll patch him in tonight."

"Let's go then, Prez." Finn smirks.

I lock the door to the clubhouse behind Finn and Cale, and follow them to the van that's parked at the end of the row of the bikes.

Finn gets in the driver's seat, I get in beside him, and Cale gets in the back with the guns.

Finn looks over the address that Nox sent me and puts the van in drive, and we roll up to the gate.

The gates slowly roll open and as we start to pull through, a car flies forward and slams on their brakes in front of us.

People surround the van with guns drawn on us and as I look around, I notice what they're wearing.

Not a-fucking-gain.

That same fucking woman with the short, brunette hair—the one who stormed my clubhouse months ago—steps out of the throng of people and taps on my window.

Glaring at her, I roll it down.

"Leave your weapons and get out of the vehicle. All of you." Her eyes land on Finn and behind me to Cale.

I run my tongue along my lip in irritation. "Are we under arrest?"

She smirks; the gloating kind of winning smirk. "Not yet, but that can change if you don't get out of the van.

24

SAINT

Cale, Finn, and I are separated and put into three different dark SUVs filled with agents. I was able to send off a quick text to Nox, telling him to abort, before I got out of the van, knowing that once we were taken in, I wouldn't be able to. The last thing I want is another brother alone in Lobo territory.

The roads are mostly clear, considering it's the middle of the night. The street lights flash by, bathing us in fleeting light. There are three agents in my vehicle, with the brunette sitting in the passenger seat; she's clearly the one in charge. The lights fade, and I realize we've left Merrill Hill.

The car is quiet the entire drive to Seattle, and we drive into an underground garage.

The agent driving opens my door for me, and I see my brothers getting out of the other vehicles. We're led to an elevator, where the lead agent uses her badge to access, and we ride it up.

My Air Forces squeak against the gray tiles that run down a plain hallway with doors placed all the way down. Oddly, we're all placed in the same interrogation room.

The door is closed behind us and I look around, but it's only a typical interrogation room. Cameras in the corners of the ceiling. An empty table, but with three chairs on side and two on the other. The room is barren, besides the table and chairs. No art on the walls, no windows, nothing.

"What the fuck is going on?" I ask, looking around.

Cale groans and falls into one of the hard, plastic chairs. "Can we get this over with? I want to go back to bed!" he yells into the room.

I take the chair on the end, leaving the one between us empty, while Finn crosses his arms and leans against the wall behind us. No matter what position Finn holds, he will always have Enforcer blood in his veins.

Fucking finally, the door opens, and I'm shocked and disheartened to see Nox walk in with the brunette leader. Damn. Getting caught up with shit is a part of the job description, but I feel bad that a Prospect is already seeing the inside of a federal interrogation room.

She takes one of the chairs on the opposite side of the table, of course, but I cock my head when Nox stands to the side of her. Why is he standing behind her like that?

"I don't believe introductions are necessary, right, Agent Brimer?" she asks, her eyes glued to me.

"No, ma'am," Nox answers, his posture straightening.

My blood runs cold in my veins, my vision turns red, and I bolt out of my chair, toppling it with the movement. "You motherfucker!" I shout, charging for Nox—*fuck* Agent Brimer.

A large hand slaps down on my shoulder and jerks me backward. Finn. "Not here, brother," he speaks next to my ear.

"Listen to your VP, Saint," the brunette says casually, watching me with calculated eyes.

I ignore her, keeping my eyes on Agent Brimer. "Fucking rat," I seethe, shaking my head.

"Let's talk about what we can do for you and the club, Saint," the other agent says. Fuck, I should really find out her name.

"Who are you?" I snap, taking my eyes off of Brimer.

"I am Special Agent in Charge Landon, and I was assigned to investigate your club for the murder of Michelle Davis."

I return to my seat, looking beside me at Cale. His story eyes are focused on Brimer as he glares death at him. Same. Fuck fake Nox.

"That shit again? You didn't find anything the first time, and your little rat didn't find anything this time either," I spit my vitriol at her. I'm fucking over this murder biting us in the fucking ass when we had nothing to do with it. I'm going to kill every last fucking Lobo for this.

She chuckles and shakes her head slightly. "Oh, Archer found a lot of things out about your club, but you're right. The Devil's Outlaws didn't kill Mrs. Davis."

My mind races with everything that *Archer* has been a part of. What conversations were carelessly spoken in front of him because we trusted him? I can't remember. My eyes dart back and forth on the table in front of me.

"I can see you racking your brain to figure out what I know." My eyes snap to hers. She leans forward with her gloating smile. "Your bullet exchange with the O'Connells. They haven't been around in a while. Murdering your girlfriend's father in New York. Your connection with Mikhail Belov. Lots of money laundering. And lastly, murdering and torturing members of Los Lobos." I swear, her smile gets wider with every act.

I lean back in my seat, keeping my mouth fucking shut. Not that I even know what the fuck to say. She has enough that she could put the whole club away.

"Luckily for you, I only want Los Lobos, and with the one you tortured confessing that they were behind Michelle's murder, you're off the hook."

"Why the fuck are we here then?" I snap.

Landon straightens in her seat, laying her hands in her lap. "We need you to abandon your revenge spree against Los Lobos. Senator Davis wants the man and his accomplices tried and prosecuted, not slaughtered in the streets."

"They killed my President and kidnapped my Old Lady." I glare at her.

Archer passes Landon a blue folder and she tosses it onto the table, sliding it across and to me. "Help us find the man who killed Michelle, and we forget everything that Agent Brimer saw and heard. Continue on your rampage, and we take everyone of you and your *Old Ladies* in."

I pick the folder up and leaf through the pages. They're detailed reports of every crime *Archer* witnessed. I shove the folder back at her and learn forward. "Leave Allie and my club out of this!"

She shrugs. "You know my terms, Saint." Special Agent Landon pushes her chair back, stands, and leaves the room without another word.

"You guys are free to go. An agent will drive you back to the clubhouse," Archer finally fucking speaks.

"Your shit better be out of my clubhouse, and I better never see you again," Finn says in an even tone, which just makes him even scarier.

"I am." Archer clasps his hands behind his back and stares straight forward. Cale and I stand and Finn leads us out of the door. "Saint." Archer places his hand on my arm, stopping me. "I don't think Los Lobos are the ones who took Allie and Peyton. There's been chatter that someone else is coming for the club."

I glance down at his fucking hand, my eyes sliding up to his. The fucking gall of this man. My tongue darts out to wet my lips, trying to tamp down my anger.

It doesn't work. In one quick motion, I cock my opposite hand back and punch him in his jaw.

Archer stumbles backward, his hand coming up to the red spot where I hit him.

We stare at each other for a moment, and then he nods. Like this makes us fucking even. Not even goddamn close.

Cale pats my shoulder and I look away from Archer and walk out of the room.

25

MASON

The table is silent.

Nobody saw that coming. Nox was an undercover agent, and he was investigating us this entire time, taking everything he learned back to his boss and ratting us out. All for a murder we had nothing to do with.

I feel like the biggest idiot in the world. It was me who looked into his background and declared him clean. It was Leo, Jack, and I who met him and brought him to the clubhouse the night of our patch in. We went out to a bar before the party, and we started talking. He seemed really cool and had the same mindset that we did, so we brought him back. We should have known he was too interested, but we just thought he was excited, like we were when we prospected. But the FBI knew that we would look into him. They knew what I went to college for, and that I'm in the club now. His alibi had to be airtight, and it was.

I'm also a little sad. I liked Nox—Archer—and I thought we could build a friendship and brotherhood.

"So that's the deal with the FBI. We need to find something to put Los Lobos away for. The murder, a RICO case, drug running, fucking anything," Saint continues.

"They're laying pretty low right now after the La Lujuria thing," Finn adds.

"You looked into that?" Saint asks, turning to face him.

Finn nods, swiping the ash off of his joint in the ashtray. "Yeah, after you told me about it, I looked into it."

"The La Lujuria thing?" Cale asks, his blonde brows pulling together.

"Los Lobos ran a high end sex club on an island in the Sound. The Vicario Cartel came in and took everyone out, and took the girls to sell into the skin market." I break my silence. I subtly look around at my brothers, checking that no one blames me for letting a spy into our home. I feel so fucking awful for that.

"Oh, fuck," Cale sighs. I leave out the part about Miles's girlfriend because I don't know if he wants that shared, or if she does.

"Alright." Saint drags his hand down his face. He got back early this morning and called everyone down here as soon as they got in; everyone's tired. "Find something before Los Lobos attack us again, but be fucking careful. We've already lost too many brothers to this shit."

We all file out of the Chapel slowly, all of us still in what we wore to bed or whatever clothes were laying on our floor that we could quickly throw on. Saint doesn't move from his chair at the head of the table.

"That's so horrible," I hear Allie say as soon as I open the door to our room.

"What's horrible?" I ask, walking to my desk and taking a seat. I start up my systems and let them get running.

She sighs and I hear her move around on the bed. "I was watching a TikTok of a mom talking about how someone hacked into her baby monitor and was talking through it."

"That's fucking sick," I say, listening to her, but also thinking of what the fuck I can do to help the club. I've been combing through known associates that could connect Los Lobos to Buxley Davis. I've gone through both of the Davis's phone records and Los Lobos' known phone records, but I don't have access to their burners, which is where the actual incriminating shit would be.

Then it comes to me, like the sun beaming down on me.

"Wait! That's it!" I shout, excited about the prospect of something promising after so many dead ends.

"Baby monitor hacking, is it? Should I be worried?" Allie asks.

"Cameras. I can check to see if the Davises had any cameras in their home and I can watch their old footage to see if I can find anything." Of course, why didn't I think of this sooner? Everyone has cameras now. I fucking work with cameras all day long. Why the hell did it take me so long to think of that!? "You're a fucking genius, Solnyshko!"

"I didn't do anything," she chuckles, and I hear her get out of bed. "But I take it since you cracked the case, you're not coming back to bed?" She wraps her arms around my shoulders and rests her chin next to my cheek.

I take one of her hands and kiss it softly. "No, babe, but Saint is taking this really hard. Maybe go find him and see if you can get him back in bed. He was in the Chapel."

She leans on me further and I delight in her warm embrace. She feels like a warm, summer breeze, wrapping you in its soft touch and soothing your soul. "Are you sure you don't need me?"

I nod and kiss her hand again. "He needs you more right now."

"Okay." She lets go and steps to the side of me. "I love you, Mason," she says, looking into my eyes.

"I love you too." I lean forward and kiss her. I love her so damn much that I've changed my entire life for her. I'd sacrifice or give up anything if it meant that she was happy, but I know she would never ask me to give up anything. Only to accept one thing. That her heart belongs to Saint as well.

It might be weird, and people definitely won't understand, but I don't give a fuck. It's not for anyone to understand. We know what feels right in our hearts. As much as I loved having Allie to myself, sharing her with Saint is a million times better.

When a woman is happy, she blooms like a flower. She's radiant and mesmerizing. She's flourished since Saint pulled his head out of his ass, and I wouldn't go back to the way it was. Not ever. It's the three of us until the end, and I'm happy with that.

26

ALLIE

I pass Cale walking up the steps with a coffee cup in one hand and a glass of orange juice in the other. He smiles a tight smile, and I get the feeling that Saint isn't the only stressed one in the club.

Peeking through the open door, I see Saint sitting in the chair at the end of the table. He's turned his chair and leans his head against the back, his blonde hair falling free around his face. His body is tight with tension and he blows out a loud breath.

Stepping in, I gently shut the door behind me. His head snaps up and his eyes focus on me.

"You should be sleeping, my Queen. The sun is barely up," he says, sitting up in his chair.

"I heard you needed me." I slowly walk around the table, keeping my eyes on him.

Saint cocks his head, watching my every move with rapture. "I always need you, Allie."

"I was hoping you would say that." I stand in front of him and look at him from above. I slowly drop to my knees in front of him, resting my hands on my knees. "I'm yours to command." I lower my eyes, hesitant to see if he'll play along.

"An obedient Allie? I never thought I'd see the day." Saint's voice turns husky. "Get my cock out and stroke me."

I shift forward, reaching for his jeans button and undoing it. I palm his dick and release it from his jeans, stroking it like he said.

"Flick your wrist at the top," he says breathlessly. Looking up at him, I try what he suggested, and his eyes burn into my soul with the molten lust that drips out of them. "Like this." He wraps his large hand around mine and directs it over his cock, showing me exactly how he likes it. My tongue traces a line along my lower lip and he tracks it with his eyes, squeezing my hand tighter around his large dick.

After a few strokes, he lets go and I continue with the way he taught me. He grows thicker in my hand, if that were even possible, and I lean down and lick along the length of him.

Saint groans above me, but I ignore him, lightly tickling my tongue down his shaft and licking back up again.

After swirling my tongue around his head a few times, I suck it into my mouth and hollow out my cheeks. I suck hard while I run my tongue along just the tip, back and forth in sweeping motions. I love the taste of Saint. He's always been sweet here, despite his sour attitude. And I love the fact that no matter how much power he has, I have the power to bring him to his knees in this moment. That's a heady feeling, having more power than the President of the deadliest motorcycle club in Washington.

What's even better? That he's mine. Along with the smartest man in the club. Saint's right, I am a fucking Queen.

Releasing slightly, I start to push my way down his cock, moving my tongue along his skin and tasting him everywhere. I'm determined to suck the stress right out of him.

He makes a little grunt and I look up at him. I completely forgot I was supposed to be submissive; the power trip took control, and I lost myself in what felt good. I just want to please him.

"Fuck, Allie. You're such a fucking whore," Saint moans. "A beautiful fucking whore." His hips stutter, jutting further into my mouth and pushing into my throat. "Deep throat me," he commands. I push further down, taking him as deep as I can. "Eyes on me," he snaps and I immediately lock eyes with him again. I start to take him into my throat, but my gag reflex causes me to pull back. "Relax your throat," Saint instructs. "When I start to enter your throat, swallow instead of restricting your throat."

Blinking, because it's not like I can nod or respond, I do as he says. I take him further into my mouth, and as he starts to get past my gag reflex and into my throat, I swallow around his cock. It feels odd and unnatural, but it works. I work down his cock, taking him in deeper and deeper.

"That's right, my Queen. Now hold still and relax." His hands slide into my hair and clasp onto the back of my head. Thats the only warning I get before he lifts his legs and starts fucking my throat.

He pounds into me, pushing deeper than I ever thought was possible. My throat constricts around him and he groans, pumping faster. Tears pool in my eyes and pour down my face. But I love this. I love that he's losing himself in me, as he always has. I love that he takes what he needs from me without an apology.

He's my destruction and I'm his salvation.

"Fuck. Fuck!" he shouts as he spills his cum down my throat. He was so deep inside of me that I didn't even need to swallow, it just trickled the rest of the way down.

His hands fall out of my hair as his hips land deftly in the chair.

I pull off of him, wiping at the saliva at the corner of my mouth with the back of my hand.

Saint leans forward and wipes the tears off of my cheeks with his thumbs.

"I love you, my Queen," Saint says, holding my cheeks. His ice blue eyes sparkle. His body has loosened and the lines in his face are gone.

"I love you too, Sainty." I smile as his face screws up.

"There's my brat." He lets go of my face, tucking himself back into his jeans while I stand up.

When I'm standing, Saint takes my hand and pulls me toward his lap. I straddle him, my arms falling on his shoulders as I look down at him.

His soft palms slide up my bare legs and rest on my hips. "I loved you being a sub today, but I like your fire more. I like it when you talk back to me."

"Oh, that's never stopping." I smirk at him, and he chuckles, squeezing my hips in his hands. "Actually, there's something I've been wanting to talk to you about."

Saint groans, dropping his head onto the back of the chair. "That's never spelled out anything good for me."

"I heard you sent Peyton to stay with Mikhail. What were you thinking, Saint?" I ask, cocking my head and waiting for his answer.

He picks his head up, all laughter and fun gone. "She was afraid to be anywhere near the club, and I don't think Mikhail is a bad guy, he just made a wrong call."

"Saint!" I chide. "He tried to have me kidnapped!"

He speaks just as the last word has left my mouth. "And if he's distracted with another girl, he won't come after you again."

I deflate slightly. I see the concern in his eyes. I would die before I left him and Mason. "But, Saint..." I whisper, trailing off.

His face relaxes again. "I promise, she's safe. I made it clear that she was free to come and go as she pleases and that I was not selling her off to him. He's just getting her out of town until she wants to come back," he says, this time his voice softer.

"Okay." I nod. "I trust you."

"Always?" he asks, his voice turning serious.

"Always," I answer. And I mean it.

27

MASON

Thirty-six hours.

That's how long I've been staring at my computer, only eating whenever Allie brings something to me and stares at me until I eat it.

I know she's worried about me. I know she stays up as long as she can at night, until she can't help but fall asleep. She stays in the room with me, bringing me water and food, but I can't stop until I've found something. We can't take any more attacks from Los Lobos. And we sure as hell can't risk the Feds reneging on their deal and hauling all of our asses in.

So I sit here, searching through the Amazon Alexa camera footage from the Davis home.

They're boring as hell. They barely talk to each other, never eat meals together, and Mrs. Davis talks mad shit about her husband to her country club friends.

They only have one Alexa in their kitchen, so I've been watching footage from that, while Miles has been watching the front door camera to see if anything flags in there. I'm hoping I can catch a conversation between her and one of her friends that might shed some light on what Buxley had to do with Los Lobos.

I find something even better—or worse, if you're Buxley Davis.

Mrs. Davis confesses to someone on the phone that she's pregnant. She said she's six weeks, and she sounds scared.

I go back in the log six weeks, and there I find exactly what I've been searching for.

One morning, after Senator Davis left for the office, Mrs. Davis was railed on the kitchen counter by a Lobo. I almost wake Allie and Saint with a girly squeal when he shows his face perfectly, not hiding it at all.

I take a screengrab of the image and pass it along to Saint, so he can get it to the Feds. We found the link between Michelle Davis and Los Lobos. All this time, we thought it was something Buxley was doing in the shadows, but it turns out it was Michelle that brought them to their doorstep.

———

TODAY IS the day of Nate's funeral. It's been a few days since I told Saint about the connection between Michelle and Los Lobos, but today isn't about that. It's about burying another of our brothers.

"Are you okay?" Allie whispers as she buttons the top button of my black shirt.

I watched her the whole time; her small hands fastening the buttons, her mint eyes focused on the task, her blond curls falling over her bare shoulders. Her silk, black slip dress hugs her curves even when it's not supposed to. She's magnificent, every day. I nod, remembering her question. "I'm okay."

She reaches behind me for my cut and pulls it up my arms, settling it on my shoulders. "We'll get through this together."

"I know." I bend down and kiss her cheek. "Where is Saint?"

Allie sighs and bites the corner of her plump, bottom lip. "Downstairs. Making sure everything is taken care of."

Saint pulls rank and orders Allie to ride with him, but I expected that. He's pretty possessive, but in a sharing kind of way—at least, most of the time. I just wish he would let us in more. I know he's struggling with losing another member. I think he lets Allie in a little bit, and I guess that's enough for now. Before Allie walks to his bike, I braid her hair and tie it off for her. It has kind of become our thing.

The sun is bright and it's hot as hell today, especially in black jeans and a black shirt, but I listen to Tobi's speech for Nate and the Priest say the prayers.

Nate's casket sinks below the grass and into the large hole in the ground, and Saint is the first to drop a peony on top of the black casket. This is too much like Ronan's funeral, and I can see ghosts dancing in Saint's eyes as he stares down at the lone flower. Stark red against the black.

It feels like an omen of all of the shit that is yet to come. This isn't over between us and Los Lobos. Not until they are in the ground or in prison. I won't accept our defeat. Not now that I finally have Allie. Not now that we have a chance to be happy together.

Saint grabs Allie's hand after, and I expect him to pull her to his bike, but he looks up from the casket and stares at me. I step up to the podium and take my flower, saying a quick prayer and crossing the flower across my chest before dropping it next to Saint's.

Taking Allie's other hand, the three of us walk toward the road, members slowly following behind us after dropping their flowers.

"Did you pass on that info?" I ask, keeping my eyes forward as we walk.

"Yeah." Saint clears his throat. "Special Agent Landon said she would look into it and get back to me."

Well, okay, I guess.

Saint stalks off toward the Chapel when we get back to the clubhouse. Leo saunters behind the bar, cranking up "I Think I'm In Love" by Kat Dahlia and starting to get drinks started for everyone lining up down the bar.

It seems to be a tradition to come back to the clubhouse and drink away our sorrows after putting a brother to rest.

For Ronan's reception, we sat around and told stories about him, drinking heavily and just being together. It's how we healed.

It looks like that's how tonight is going to go as well.

"I'm worried about him," Allie says softly, curling into my side.

I look down at her beautiful face. Her eyes crinkle as she watches Saint walk away. "Go to him then, Solnyshko." I incline my head toward his retreating back.

Allie shakes her head, her blonde curls brushing over my hand on her shoulder. "We should go together. It's the three of us, right?"

She's right. We share more than just a club now, I should be there for him too. "Let's grab drinks first." I lead Allie toward the bar, tucking her farther under my arm.

Walking behind Allie, I carry the drinks for Saint and I. "I'm not really sure what to say to him, Solnyshko," I admit. I guess we just sit and listen to him talk through his feelings? Would he even do that?

Allie looks over her shoulder, shaking her head. "No words tonight." She turns back around with that cryptic message and pushes one of the double doors open, stepping inside and leaving it open for me to follow.

"What is this? A meeting of the kinky fucks?" Saint snarks,

slouching deeply in his chair and staring at the wall where a picture of the club hangs.

"Quit avoiding your feelings, Saint," Allie says, walking past the row of empty chairs.

He turns to look only at her, because she's the axis of our world, and says, "If I let myself feel this too, I'll finally drown."

Allie shrugs, stepping in front of him. "Then drown, Saint. I've always been there to save you."

Saint's eyes drift over to me, waiting at the middle of the table. "And you just had to bring Underwood." He rolls his eyes, but they lack the cutting edge he usually uses.

"He's a part of this. It's all or nothing," Allie answers.

Saint nods, holding Allie's eyes. Sighing, he finally speaks again. "Up on the table, my Queen. Let me drown in your ocean."

Allie slides between the arm of Saint's chair and the table, and he turns to face her. With his hands squeezing her hips, he lifts her onto the table and she lands with a soft thump.

Pulling out my chair, I take a seat and slide down into the chair, spreading my legs wide. I'm intrigued to watch what's about to happen. Excited, even.

Saint's hand slides up Allie's stomach and stops between her breasts. He pushes her down against the table and when she's laying flat, she turns her head to smile at me. Her blonde hair fans out around her head like water and her smile lights up the already bright room. Sunlight shines in from the window behind Saint and illuminates Allie like she's an angel.

Saint's hands travel up her thighs and push her black dress over her hips.

He strips her panties down her legs and stuffs them into the inside pocket of his cut before leaning down and licking a slow line up her pussy.

Allie arches her neck, throwing her head back and groaning.

Saint lifts her legs and rests them over his shoulders as he slides the chair closer to her.

Watching Saint eat out our girl is almost as great as doing it myself, but more than anything, I just enjoy watching Allie get off. The small twitches of her body, the noises she makes, the way her muscles clench and release. I miss some of these things when I'm the one bringing her pleasure.

She moves her head wildly between Saint and I, like she doesn't know where to look. Her pupils are blown, almost completely eclipsing her mint green eyes.

Saint slurps, licks, and sucks. The wet noises Allie's pussy makes are obscene, and the sexiest thing I've ever heard. Allie sucks in sharp breaths, moans, groans, and whispers Saint's name.

Reaching down, I unbutton my jeans and pull my cock out, pumping it while I watch Saint eat out Allie. Saint notices and motions for me to stand up.

"Let her watch you jack yourself," he says between licks, lazily pumping two fingers inside of Allie.

Doing as I'm told, I stand and stroke my cock slowly. Allie's eyes trace the movement of my hand, squirming as Saint's mouth suctions to her clit once more.

Her delicate hand reaches toward me, and I step closer to her, letting her wrap her hand around me and take over.

She squeezes me tightly as I rock my hips into her hand, my head falling forward to watch her every move. She's so fucking perfect, laying here between us.

"Ah!" she moans. "Saint, I'm going to cum." Her head snaps down to Saint.

He pulls away immediately. "Not yet, my Queen." He smiles confidently as Allie lets go of me and groans.

He flips her over and brings her closer to the edge of the table, handling her like she's a doll.

"Saint Viotto!" Allie snaps, lifting onto her elbows and turning around to look at him. Her scolding halts when she sees him pushing his jeans and boxers down, his erect cock springing free.

"Lay down and open wide, Allie." His eyes drill into hers and she turns around without another word. He handles her so roughly, but she loves it. Him and I are complete opposites. I'm the tender touch and he's the demanding order.

Allie smirks up at me and she opens her mouth for me. Saint lifts his leg and settles in behind Allie, guiding his cock toward her pussy.

Immediately, I shove my cock in Allie's mouth, and she chuckles around me, but as Saint sinks deeply into her, she moans for a long time.

My balls seize up and I almost cum right there, but that's the reason I hastily shoved my cock in her mouth—to be able to feel the moan she was inevitably going to release.

Saint wastes no time. As soon as he's balls deep, he pounds into her relentlessly. His fingers dig into her hips and ass and he loses himself in her.

Allie tries to suck me, but as Saint pounds into her, she can't help but give in to the pleasure and lose herself as well.

I end up taking over and fucking her mouth, which isn't any less enjoyable.

My fingers tangle in her hair and she stares up at me. She opens her throat for me and I slide into it, her nose brushing against my skin as I push in all the way.

Allie's eyes glaze over as Saint and I fuck her hard. Her nails dig into my ass and it feels like she lets out one continuous moan, the vibration in her throat never stopping.

I look up right as Saint sticks two fingers in Allie's pussy, alongside his cock.

He pulls them out and they glisten in the light, then he spreads the wetness around Allie's asshole and slides into it.

Allie's moans quicken, the heavy breaths leaving her nose pick up and tickle me.

"Harder," I say to Saint.

I can feel in the way she's breathing that she's close to cumming, and I want to be right there with her when she does.

Saint's fingers and hips pick up and the slaps of his hips hitting her ass echo around the room. He starts to grunt as he moves more on top of her and pounds into her at, frankly, an impressive speed.

Saint's breath stutters and I know he's about to cum, but so am I, so I pull out of Allie's mouth and quickly stroke my cock until I shoot my cum all over her open mouth and face.

Allie's eyes are closed in pure bliss as she fights to suck in deep breaths and tries to moan out her pleasure through her orgasm. Her entire body trembles as she cums around Saint's cock, and he grunts alongside her.

I will never forget this in my entire life. Sharing her for the first time was life altering, but getting to watch her up close, take in her every breath and move, was new for me. Usually, I'm more focused on bringing her pleasure than actually enjoying her pleasure.

As her breathing slows and Saint pulls out of her, his cock wet with her cum, she inclines her head toward me. "I can't believe you came on my face," she chuckles.

"Shit," I laugh, looking at the creamy ropes dripping down her face. "I thought I might choke you if I came in your mouth while you were moaning so much." I quickly drop my cut on the table next to her and pull my shirt over my head. Kneeling down in front of her, I wipe away my cum with my shirt. "You're probably going to need to wash your face." I laugh, examining her ruined makeup and cleaning up the last remaining rope on her cheek.

"More like I'm going to need to shower." She finally opens her eyes when I pull my shirt away. They're so bright, and so much love radiates out of them.

"I think we might be able to help you with that," Saint says, leaning down and kissing her bare ass cheek.

28

SAINT

Loose gravel crunches under the tires of my bike as I pull into the rundown bar at the edge of Oak River. Why the fuck Special Agent Landon asked me to meet her all the way out here, I have no idea.

Oak River is over an hour away from Merrill Hill, a tiny, old town at the base of the mountains.

Men drinking the day away turn their heads, their eyes narrowing on me as I walk past them and into the wood-paneled bar.

The bar is half full with locals, "Paranoid" by Chase Atlantic plays over the radio, and I look around the room for the brunette.

Unfortunately, she's not here, but her fucking lackey is. I spot the back of Archer's head sitting at the bar.

Rolling my eyes, I stomp over to him. "Your boss said I was meeting her."

He stays looking forward, lifting his hand to signal the bartender. "I asked to be the one to talk to you."

"Why?" I snap, shooing away the girl when she comes over to take my order.

Fake Nox licks his lips. "I wanted to apologize. I go under all the time, but this time was different. I really did bond with your club," he says softly.

"I'm fucking sure." I ignore him. "What the fuck did you guys want?"

Archer's eyes shift around the room. "We took in Los Lobos, and I have someone I think you should talk to."

I shake my head. "Look, I understand why you all wanted to get them so badly, but why not just let the Cartel take care of them? They were already halfway there anyway."

He takes a swig from his bottle. "There's a lot more going on with Los Lobos and the Vicario Cartel than you know. Los Lobos are also a lot bigger than you think. Your intel is either old or wrong, they could have easily taken your club on if we hadn't stepped in."

I roll my eyes. Nox wasn't this annoying, but now that he's Archer, I just want to punch him again. "Who do you think I need to talk to? I just want to be done with you and your boss. I held up my end of the deal."

Archer slams the rest of his beer, tossing a twenty onto the counter and standing. "Which is why I'm rewarding you."

I look around. People pretend not to watch us, but I can feel their secretive glances. "Why did you have me meet you here?" Archer looks around, noticing the eyes as well, and it becomes clear. "You motherfucker. You're using me for your next job aren't you?"

Archer shrugs, no amount of remorse for using me. "Nothing says shady like a meeting with the President of the most powerful biker gang in the state."

Glaring, I step up to him, our chests bumping together. "I should beat your ass right here and tell everyone who you are."

Archer holds my eyes. The obedient Prospect is a thing of the past. "Maybe, but then I'd take you in for obstructing a

Federal investigation, and you wouldn't ever find out who really kidnapped Allie and Peyton."

I chuckle, but there isn't a speck of humor in it. "Los Lobos kidnapped them."

Archer shakes his head. "That's who they wanted you to think took them." He knocks his shoulder against mine, pushing past me. "Now, come on."

I don't have a choice, I have to follow him. There is no world in which Allie's kidnappers are able to go free. I thought we had killed the ones working for Los Lobos that were holding Allie, and when I found out the FBI wanted them, I knew I wouldn't get my revenge, but at least they wouldn't be walking free.

Whoever did this to my girl cannot be allowed to walk free. I won't allow it.

In the parking lot, Archer gets into a sleek, black Camaro. He waits for me to get on my bike and then he pulls out onto the road and guns it.

We pass through the town in under two minutes. Maybe less. And he pulls into the driveway of a modest two story home with a large, wrap around porch.

"I thought you were trying to be sketchy? This neighborhood doesn't exactly fit your cover, does it?" I ask, swinging my leg over my bike as he shuts the door to his Camaro.

Archer pins me with an unamused look. "You don't need to worry about my assignment."

"No, I just need to worry about why you brought me all the way out to Oak River."

"She's inside." He gestures toward the red front door.

He takes the steps two at a time and crosses over the wide porch. I follow him.

"Miss Smith! I brought that friend I told you about," Archer calls as he steps into the house.

I walk inside and stand beside him. A vaguely familiar

woman steps around the corner of the kitchen and into the living room. Long, jet-black hair, piercing, blue eyes, thick lashes, and tattoos running down one arm. "Reyna?" I ask, my eyes switching between the woman we saved and Archer.

She clears her throat, lifting her chin. "I wasn't completely honest with you when you rescued me from La Lujuria."

"What's going on?" I take a step backwards, readying myself for anything at this point.

"I worked for Los Lobos at La Lujuria. I know who all of the members are. They weren't the ones who took me and Allie." She blinks her eyes innocently.

"Why did you lie in the helicopter then?" I ask. I don't know what to think, but this doesn't sound right.

"Can we sit?" she asks, motioning to the couch.

I look between Archer and Reyna again. "Go, Saint. Reyna will explain everything."

I follow Reyna to the couch, and she takes the armchair beside it. Archer sits on the landing of the brick fireplace across from me.

Taking a moment, I look around the place. It's minimally furnished with boxes sitting around, some opened and some not. It looks like he just got here.

"I was the top earner for La Lujuria, so when the Cartel came, my boss, Hector, took me with him. That's how I got out of the massacre. Los Lobos and the Kings of Mayhem weren't working together at first. But the Kings found out that Los Lobos killed that woman, so the Kings promised Los Lobos your territory if they helped take your club out. Los Lobos were supposed to distract you while the Kings moved in. Your President was figuring it all out, so one of the Kings' girls contacted him and said she had information for him. It was a trap, and Los Lobos took out your President that night. They are the ones who took Allie. Los Lobos lived out their usefulness and the Kings came to kill Hector and that's when they took me too. They said they were tying up loose ends and shot him right in front of me. They were going to try to sell me and Allie into the skin market. They wanted to cripple you."

"How do you know all of this?" I ask, skeptical. Why would a whore know the inner workings of not one, but two gangs?

Reyna holds my eyes the entire time. She's not the scared girl she was back on that island. "I was Miguel's favorite, and he got real chatty after he blew his load. He would tell me of how much money and power he would have after he helped the Kings take you out. He wanted me to leave the club to be with him."

"Why should I believe the word of a sex worker? Or the lust-filled bragging of a dead man?" I cock my head, staring her down.

"He said the Kings sent spies in the beginning to watch over you, but they never got anything. Miguel took one of them in after you guys caught him. You fucked him up pretty badly. He died later that night on Miguel's kitchen table."

The Brother's Coalition. Mother fuckers.

"Why did you lie to us?"

She looks at Archer. He nods and she turns back to me. "I was scared. I didn't know who you were, but when Agent Brimer picked up all of Los Lobos, they found me too. Agent Brimer said you would protect me if I told you everything I knew about the Kings."

I look ahead at Archer. "I'm not a fucking halfway house."

"Saint," he chides. "She'll be dead if the Kings or Los Lobos find out she helped you."

"Fine, but only until Los Lobos are locked up and the Kings are gone," I concede. She did help today, and I know Allie has a soft spot for her since they were being held together. She was already ready to kill me over Peyton, she really will do it this time if she finds out I abandoned Reyna. "You're bringing her to the clubhouse. And don't come in, just drop her at the gate and get the fuck out of our lives."

He nods, standing at the same time I do. "I'll drop her off tonight."

I look at Reyna one last time before I turn back to Archer. "You bringing me this information doesn't make us even."

"I know." He looks down for a moment. "But if you need a favor in the future, you can reach out and I'll do what I can."

"Fuck off," I sigh, turning around and leaving this shit hole town.

29

SAINT

"So, that's the plan?" Tobi asks, his age-weathered fingers steepled in front of his face.

I don't take Tobi's questions as challenging me. I know that's not his intention, he just has to know every single angle of a plan so he can understand it. That's why I'm not upset when he's always the first to speak after something has been laid out. "Do you see anything wrong with it?" I cock my head, waiting for his approval or suggestions.

Pursing his lips, he shakes his head. "No."

I look around at all of my brothers, and each one has their undivided attention on me. On our plan to end this shit once and for all. "Does *anyone* have a problem with it?" No one says anything, and some shake their heads. "Alright, I already called Killian, he's bringing what we need." Sighing, I shove away from the table. "Go say your goodbyes, we'll leave after we have everything."

Chairs scrape the wood floor as everyone pushes away from the table. "Wait. Leo, Jack, I need a minute."

Leo and Jack look between each other while the others file out of the room, Finn closing the door as the last one out.

"I've let it go unattended for too long, and I want you both to manage Second," I say, watching the both of them.

Leo smirks. Of course he does. "You're putting us in charge of a strip club?"

I roll my eyes. This is the right choice, I know it is, but it doesn't mean it isn't going to come with Leo sized headaches. "Everyone else is already doing something for the club."

"Not the oldies," Leo challenges.

"Tobi is useless right now and Wyatt has one foot halfway out of the club as it is. I'm not putting more stress on either of them." I narrow my eyes at Leo, praying for him to shut the fuck up for once. "I'm giving you the opportunity to show me that you can take something more seriously than how many times you can get your dick wet in a week."

"You got it, Prez. We'll go in tomorrow before opening to look over the books and the club," Jack pipes in. Thank fuck.

"Ask Huntley to take a look at the books and teach you both what you need to know. We've lost a few strippers recently so you'll also need to hire some new girls." I sigh again and push up from my chair. I need a fucking break, but that's not going to happen tonight.

In the bar, Mason has our girl under his arm, her arms wrapped around his stomach tightly. He's whispering something into her hair as her eyes wander around the room before stopping on me.

She pulls me to her like a lighthouse on a stormy night. She leads me to her with the promise of safety. She's my lighthouse. My refuge. My solace. My light.

"I don't like saying goodbye to you both like this," Allie says as she steps out from under Mason's arms and into mine.

"I know, my Queen." I hug her tightly, squeezing her into my chest. "I wish I could say this will be the last time..." I trail off, not wanting to finish the sentence.

"I know," she says softly. "Look out for each other." Her eyes bounce between Mason and I.

"We will." Mase closes the gap between us and hugs her from behind, placing a gentle kiss to the back of her head.

"Prez!" Leo calls. "Everyone's here." He points his thumb behind him to the door.

Nodding, I call him off. I look back at Allie, taking her face in my hands and pressing our foreheads together. "We will come back to you. If it's the last thing I do, I will make sure we both come back to you tonight."

Tears fill her eyes, but she holds them back and nods. I kiss her one last time before letting her go so she can tell Mason goodbye.

Outside, Killian stands beside his classic Maserati with Conor opening the trunk. Miles sits on the hood of his Porsche, holding a glinting silver skull mask in his hand.

I release a heavy breath and make my way to Killian and Conor. Killian meets me at the back of the car. "We brought everything you asked for."

I scan over the contents of the trunk, the low lighting shining down on them, mentally ticking items off of my checklist. "Thank you for coming." I look up at Ronan's cousin. They look nothing alike, and it makes this easier.

Killian chews on the inside of his lip before speaking. "Anything for Ro."

"They weren't the ones who killed him, but they were helping them." I step backwards and Killian slams the trunk closed.

Turning around, I nod at Mase, who's talking to Miles. He gives me a nod back, and I motion for everyone to get going.

Mason, Jack, Leo, and I get in Mason's truck. Cale, Finn, Wyatt, and Tobi take Cale's Raptor. And Killian, Conor, and Miles take their own vehicles.

I wanted us to arrive as stealthily as possible, so no loud bikes, no suspicious vans. Just our personal vehicles that people won't connect to us as easily.

We all load up, and then we're off on the two hour ride to the Kings' clubhouse.

This ends tonight. For the last fucking time.

———

WE PARK two miles from the Kings' cliffside clubhouse. We all file out and suit up. Bulletproof vests, night vision goggles, ARs, AKs, knives, and a shit ton of ammo. Leo and Jack are put in charge of carefully carrying Conor's homemade bombs. The moon is high in the sky as we hike the rest of the way through the thick forest that surrounds the clubhouse. Maybe the Kings had the right idea by putting their clubhouse outside of town in a secluded area, instead of on the outskirts of town like ours is. Mason pulls his hood over his head as we walk through the trees and the soft earth, Finn turns his ball cap forward to hang over his face, and Leo pulls a black bandana over his nose and mouth. The creepiest, though, is Miles's shining silver skull mask.

We slowly and very meticulously make our way through the woods. We have to make sure we don't trip some booby trap wire or get caught on any kind of camera or sensor. It's imperative that they don't know we're coming. Our plan will only work if they have no idea we're here until it's too late for them.

Once we reach the treeline on the side of the clubhouse, we set up on our stomachs and survey the grounds with night vision binoculars. There are a few people mingling around outside, around a fire, but they're at the front of the building, so they shouldn't be a problem for us.

Conor starts pulling out the small bombs and when I give

him the signal, he takes off into the clearing and around the backside of the clubhouse. Killian said he was the best choice to place the bombs, and I trusted him. He wouldn't put his cousin in danger if he didn't think he could hold his own.

We wait with baited breath until Conor sneakily runs around the corner of the building and books it toward us.

The minute he hits the soil beside us, a loud boom erupts from the clubhouse and smoke starts to rise from the kitchen in the back of the building.

The small explosion does exactly what it was supposed to do.

Everyone inside the clubhouse hurries outside, half asleep, half naked, and completely unaware.

Without hesitation, we open fire. Kings fall one by one, until they get their wits about them and take cover.

Now we'll take the fight to them.

They're unarmed for the most part, so it shouldn't be all that difficult.

Jack, Killian, and Conor stay behind with their long guns and scopes, but the rest of us push off of our stomachs and rush into the clearing.

The Kings meet us halfway and the real fun begins.

Skull's eyes laser focus on me and he charges at me, a sneer plastered across his face. Smiling, I shove my handgun in the back of my jeans and lift my fists. I don't want this over quickly for him. I'm going to savor this, because this is as good a revenge as I'm going to get for Ronan, and he deserves so much worse than a bullet for taking my woman.

He swings at me and I dodge him, bouncing back on my back foot and avoiding his fist. We do this a few times, turning in a circle while I study his patterns. His footwork. His attitude and lack of patience. He's getting irritated, and he's going to snap soon.

I take my opening and swing, connecting with his jaw and sending him staggering backward. I use this opportunity to pounce, taking him to the ground and pummeling his face.

I use every ounce of strength, every bit of rage that I wallowed in for the last two months. I vent it all on his face. Over and over, my fists pound into him.

His arms snake up with the last of his will and clamp around my throat, squeezing with his last remaining might.

I hit harder, aiming for his temple and using my elbow to smash in his nose and cheeks.

As I'm about to run out of air, his hands lose their strength and deftly drop from my neck, landing next to him on the bloodied grass.

I don't even look at him, just roll over and land next to him as I suck down deep lungfuls of air.

The fight continues all around me and my eyes land on Miles as he cuts through a King's throat, deep red blood splattering across his skull mask. That shit is creepy as fuck. But then he drops to his knees and I sit up quickly, worried that he's injured.

But he's not. He presses his hands over a wound on a body.

Tobi's body.

I crawl to them, blood seeping out of a wound on Tobi's chest and slithering through Miles's fingers.

I press two bloodied fingers against Tobi's neck, watching his glossed over eyes that stare straight toward the dark sky, and I already know before my fingers hit his skin. He's gone.

"I'm sorry, Saint," Miles says from behind the mask. "I got to him as soon as I could."

I shake my head, pulling my fingers away. I was right next to him and I didn't even hear the gunshot. "Just go end this shit," I snap.

We weren't supposed to lose anyone else.

I sit with Tobi as the fight continues. Girls run screaming down the road. We didn't want to hurt them, so we ignored them.

Anytime anyone came near me, Miles fought them off, taking them down with his blade.

Eventually, everyone gathers around, some standing, others sitting with me. Even Killian and Conor emerge from the trees with Jack and settle around me.

We sit there for a while. The night is quiet now and the moon shines brightly across the bloodstained grass.

"Leave everyone where they lay and let's take Tobi home," I say, pushing up off of the ground. Cale, Finn, and Jack carry Tobi to Mason's truck.

I walk around the bodies, looking at every face. One is missing.

I grab Leo's arm as he walks past me. "Where's Colter?" I ask.

"Bad news, Prez." Leo licks his lips. "He jumped off the cliff and took off in a speedboat. I would have gone over the edge with him but I didn't think he'd survive the drop."

I look around at the clubhouse that has now filled with flames, the thick smoke billowing into the dark sky. This place is in shambles. The entire club is dead.

"It's fine, he won't be back." I turn around and start for the truck, but Wyatt stops me.

His eyes sparkle with unshed tears. "I need to talk to you, Prez," he says in his gruff voice.

"I'm really sorry about Nate and Tobi, Wyatt," I say. They were his best friends, Ronan too. He's lost just as much as I have. He hurts just as deeply.

"They were good men," he grunts.

I nod. "They were," I agree.

Wyatt clears his throat. "I would like to put in a vote to transfer."

I lick my lip. I was expecting something like this. "Where do you want to go?" I ask.

"Down to the California chapter. I've been talking to Sketch and they need some help making the ghost guns and running them." He looks away and I see a tear slip down his face before he swipes it away. "I can't be here anymore." He looks at me again. "I'm surrounded by ghosts everywhere I look."

I nod and pull him into a hug. It feels strange. I don't know if I've ever hugged a brother besides Ronan, and Wyatt is a huge guy. He limply wraps his arms around me, and that's how I know that he needs to get the hell out of here. "I understand, brother. We'll vote on it tomorrow, but no one will vote against you."

Calm. That's how I would describe the last two weeks.

Wyatt left the day after Tobi's funeral. Mase, Leo, and Jack went with him to California and spent a few days with him there. They said he looked much better in the California sunshine. More at peace. I hope they're right.

I didn't know him well, but I could see the change in him after Nate died. It only got worse with Tobi's death.

Although things have been calm, we've also been busy. Everyone was finally able to move out of the clubhouse, and Saint and I had a lot of work to do on his master bedroom after he destroyed it. He still won't tell me why he did it, but I know Saint and I know he has outbursts.

Mason and I moved into Saint's house, and since Sophie and Logan have been practically living together the last two months, I decided to sell my house in Merrill Hill, and my dad's brownstone in New York. I don't want anything to do with him anymore, and these were the last things connecting me to him.

My life is perfect. I've never felt more loved, or loved anyone this much. I love coming home from work in the evenings, cooking with Saint, and sitting in the backyard, eating with both of my men. I love having everyone over on Sundays and having club dinners, because I told Saint I wanted to continue to do that. Reyna has even been coming to the dinners, since she lives at the clubhouse now.

Saint said she helped with who kidnapped us, so the club is taking care of her. I like that.

Even though we didn't spend much time together, I feel connected to her because we shared that horror together.

Huntley has actually been getting closer with Reyna, and I think I see a friendship blooming between them. They're a good fit. They're both intimidatingly beautiful, and they have harsh personalities, but I think they understand each other in a way that no one else does.

Saint said things should be safer now, that everyone that was after us is gone. I don't want to know exactly what he means by that, but since he was loading up guns the last time the club left and they came back with a dead member, I can pretty much guess what happened.

"What are you thinking about, Solnyshko?" Mason's voice startles me and I use the bluetooth remote that I'm holding to turn down the song playing through the speakers in our bedroom: "moon and back" by JVKE.

"Just looking for orcas," I answer, looking out the large window as Mason's arms wrap around me from behind.

He rests his chin on my shoulder and whispers in my ear, "You know that they're the bullies of the sea, right?"

I chuckle, leaning my cheek against his. "They're just misunderstood."

He hums as he steps around me and pulls me into his chest. He smells like the fresh air outside, and I take a deep breath to keep him with me forever. To keep this moment with me forever.

"Please say yes," he whispers.

"What?" I pull away, narrowing my eyes.

Mason answers by moving his big hands to my shoulders and spinning me around.

Saint is kneeling in front of me with a small, black box in his hand. "You have two weeks before school starts. I think we should spend it in Singapore."

"Why Singapore?" I ask, my eyes flitting between him and the box.

"Because there, you can marry both of us," he answers, popping open the ring box. Nestled inside is the most beautiful ring I've ever seen. A large, oval diamond and an aquamarine teardrop stone sit side by side on a plain, silver band.

A pure, white diamond to represent Saint, and a stone the color of Mason's eyes to represent him.

Tears fill my eyes as I extend my left hand to Saint. "I couldn't imagine a more perfect life than one with the two of you." I turn to look over my shoulder at Mason as well.

Saint slides the ring onto my finger, and it's a perfect fit. "Show us how much you want to be our wife then, my Queen."

"Right here?" I ask, sliding the thin strap of my slip dress over my shoulder.

"The only place you belong is between the two of us," Mason answers, taking the other strap and pulling it down my other shoulder.

The thin, silk dress falls to the floor in a puddle.

Saint's warm hands glide up my thighs, his fingers slipping under my lace panties and hooking around them. With a sinful look in his eyes, he slowly pulls them down my legs.

"Hold her open for me, Mason," Saint says, smirking while he bites his lip.

Mase chuckles behind me as he bends down and hefts me

into his arms, his hands snaking under my thighs and opening them. I yelp, scared that he's going to drop me—but, of course, he's not—it's Mason. My arm clamps around his neck and I hold onto him to keep my back steady against his chest.

Saint licks a ring around my asshole before moving to my pussy and spreading my lips open. His mouth suctions onto my clit and he sucks hard. He's not easing me into anything, but that's Saint. He's not gentle in any way, especially not with me.

Mason and Saint hold me in an iron grip, not letting me move at all, and all I can do is let Saint have his way with me.

Just when I think I'm about to pass out from pleasure, Saint moves from my clit to my leaking center. "I gotta make sure this beautiful pussy is wet enough for the both of us," he says before he plunges his tongue inside of me and fucks me with it. His nose rubs against my clit, and I groan, resting my head against Mason's shoulder.

"This isn't fair," I plead.

Mason laughs, his chest shaking me and making everything Saint is doing below so much better. "You're the one who wanted two husbands. Get ready for a lifetime of this."

With my left hand, I reach down and weave my fingers through Saint's hair. He immediately pulls away from me and takes my hand, staring down at my ring.

"Fuck," he curses. "I can't wait any longer. I need to be inside of my wife." He quickly stands and starts undoing his jeans.

"I'm not your wife yet," I laugh.

"It doesn't matter." He shakes his head. "You've been mine since I saw you in that coffee shop. He grabs my waist as Mason still holds me and pushes inside of me. "I don't love making eye contact with Underwood while I fuck you, but goddamn, you feel so fucking perfect squeezing me."

"Saint," I moan, my pussy already fluttering around him.

But before Saint can start thrusting, Mason lifts me slightly and drops me down onto Saint's dick, making me ride Saint as he holds me wide open.

Saint's and my eyes go wide, and Mason continues as Saint and I stay still, letting him set the pace of our bodies.

"Oh, God," I groan, staring into Saint's ice blue eyes.

"Fuck, you're flooding me, my Queen. It's now or never, Mase," Saint chokes out.

Mason stops. "Take her and I'll get the lube." I never thought I would love a sentence more before I had two fiancés.

I don't feel complete until they're both filling me. Being between them, our bodies slick with sweat and lube, is the most wonderful place imaginable. I feel more loved than I ever have in my life. I feel like the sexiest woman that ever existed. I feel like I could rule the world if I convinced two possessive men to share one woman. Me.

I don't need anything for the rest of my life. All I want is Saint and Mason.

Saint and Mason shuffle me between them, and I wrap my arms around Saint. He carries me to our bed and lays down on his back.

"Ride me, my Queen." Saint settles against the pillow beneath his head.

Sitting up, I cock my brow. "Am I going to have to make myself cum too, because you haven't done that yet either." I sink down on his cock, waving my hips back and forth.

Saint's eyes flick behind me before answering. "We're about to blow your fucking mind, Allie, so get this pretty pussy nice and ready for us."

The bed dips behind us and Mason's hand rests on my hip. "I need you to tell me if it's too much, okay?"

Sinking back down on Saint's dick, I look over my shoulder. "We've done this before, Mase. I'm fine."

"Not like this, Solnyshko." He shakes his head. "Do you trust us?" His eyes bore into mine.

"Without a doubt," I answer honestly, staring right back at him.

He nods once, his smiling lighting up the already bright room. "Then lean forward and relax."

Doing as he says, I rest against Saint's chest and place small kisses to it.

I jump a little when I feel Mason smear the chilly lube to my pussy. That's not where that goes, but maybe he thinks I'll need it.

Then I feel the head of his cock press against my opening. Right alongside Saint's.

"Oh my God." I suck in a breath and Mason stops.

Saint's hands gently run up and down my sides. "Do you think this perfect pussy can fit us both?"

"Do you want me to stop, Solnyshko?" Mason asks.

"No." I shake my head, making my body relax again. I was taken off guard, but I am curious to try this.

Mason slowly works his slippery cock inside of me. We take it slow, moving only small increments at a time, and when he's finally full seated, I feel like I'm going to burst open.

And then they start moving.

Stars burst in front of my eyes, my vision completely blacking out while they fuck me.

"Fuck, she's already cumming," Saint grunts, his hips thrusting harder.

I can't make any noise; every muscle is tensed as I cum harder than I ever have in my life. My voice doesn't work, my vision doesn't work, I can't move my body. But it's amazing.

"She's not stopping. I'm gonna bust," Mason groans, his thrusts never faltering.

"Amateur," Saint says under his breath.

I don't know how long they last. It feels like a lifetime and too short of a time all in one. I don't know if I have multiple consecutive orgasms or if it is one continuous one, but I know that I never stop cumming the entire time they fuck me.

Saint finishes first. "Fuck, fuck," he groans. "I'm out."

Mason chuckles, lifting my hips, and Saint slips out, his soaked cock slapping against his abs. "Who's the amateur now?"

Mason leans down over me, compacting me between the two of them. "Just lay here and be my little fuck doll, Solnyshko," Mason's husky voice whispers in my ear.

His hands press into my lower back as he lifts himself and angles himself inside of me. He pummels into me and Saint takes my chin and leads me to his lips.

Saint's tongue traces along my lips before I open up to him and he dives deep into me. He fucks my mouth with his tongue while Mason fucks my pussy.

"That's my good fucking girl," Mason shouts as his hot cum shoots deep inside of me.

He pulls out and places kisses up my back while Saint pulls away from my mouth. "Thank you for saving me, Allie."

Leo

"I CAN'T BELIEVE Saint just put us in charge of Second and then left the country to get married," I say, leaning back in the chair in front of the stage.

Auditions for new talent start in twenty minutes and I'm ready to see some fresh girls walk through that door. The kinky cut sluts and faux, innocent college girls are getting stale.

"I don't blame him. He needed some time away after all that shit went down," Jack hums from the seat next to me.

He is right. The two guys that took it the hardest were Saint and Wyatt, and now they're both gone. Wyatt more permanently than Saint, but still. "It doesn't feel right though, does it? That it all ended so easily?" I ask, looking at the empty bar. The only other people here are the house mom and a bartender hanging at the bar.

"It wasn't easy," he counters, sounding annoyed. "Ronan, Tobi, and Nate died. You had the shit beat out of you at that clubhouse. We were being investigated for a murder we didn't have shit to do with, and Allie and Peyton were kidnapped." He lets out a frustrated breath and crosses his arms, staring ahead.

I side eye him and wait for him to calm down a little. I know I hit a nerve. "You're right, and I know you had a crush on Peyton."

"I did not have a crush on Peyton. She was just the only girl who wasn't constantly trying to fuck an Outlaw." He rolls eyes.

I'll back off for now, but I know he's lying. "Do you ever regret it?" I ask quietly, hesitantly. "Regret joining the club?"

Jack finally turns to look at me, but it's quick. "No." He looks forward again at the empty stage. "It's what I had to do."

Even after everything we've been through, his walls are still so high with me. He knows everything about me—he knows me better than I know myself—but a lot of him is still a mystery to me.

Regardless of all of that, he's still the best friend I've ever had. I've never had someone look out for me or care for me the way he does. He just has his own way of showing it.

The front door opens, letting in the bright light from outside. A sexily curvy body walks in, backlit from the sun and only showing her blacked out silhouette.

She's hired. I don't give a fuck if she can dance, she'll learn. And with a body like that, the guys won't care while she does.

The door slams shut a moment later, cutting the sunlight, and her face comes into view.

My heart stops in my chest and my throat starts to close up, just like the first time I saw her.

To be continued...

ACKNOWLEDGMENTS

We're halfway through this series. Only two more Outlaws to go until the end. And it's rather fitting that I'm writing this acknowledgment on the one year anniversary of Only The Strong, though you won't read this until later this month.

I've written a lot of words this year, fought with a lot of characters. I've cried and laughed and wished I could hug some of these fake people that live in my mind. I hope you connect with my characters as much as I do, and that they help you deal with every day life as they help me.

OBAM was the hardest book for me to write yet, and I'm not sure why. I guess a lot of it was mental blocks, but we're finally here at the end.

I would like to thank my alpha reader and best friend, Kiersten, for always encouraging me and telling me I rock when I feel like giving up. You always have the best advice, and I couldn't make half of the decisions I do without you! You are the reason this book is making it into the world. Thank you endlessly. I love you.

Thank you to my readers, you are the reason that I get to write these stories that honestly keep my sane. I hope you continue to believe in my stories, and I hope that I get to keep sharing my thoughts with you.

Bethany

ABOUT THE AUTHOR

To discuss spoilers, theories, cliffhanger rants, and read deleted scenes for Will Survive, join our Facebook group, The DO Chapel.

You can also follow me on TikTok @queenb17, Instagram @bethanydawnauthor, and my Facebook page @BethanyDawnAuthor

ALSO BY BETHANY DAWN

The Devil's Outlaws

Only The Strong

Will Survive

This Mess

Of Bikes and Men

Outlaws Never Die (January 2024)

The Devil Always Wins (May 2024)

The Devil Didn't Want Me (September 2024)

A Devil's Forever (December 2024)

One Night

A Night With My Best Friend

Doxed Duet

Doxed (November 2023)